A Gay Affair

By
Robert Lee Reynolds

Imagination Press, LLC
Editors:
Doc Wilson
Teresa Hamilton

A Gay Affair

First Edition
Printed in the United States of America
ISBN:978-0-692-61744-1

Dedication Page

To my grandson Rajun, who demonstrated the courage to express his preference without fear or prejudice from others. His unconditional love for even those who disagree with his choice and lifestyle is commendable.

I love you,

Pop.

To my gay co-workers' that I served with in security in Baltimore, Maryland, thanks for teaching me that gay people are just that, PEOPLE! You taught me how to dismantle homophobia, and embrace new friends. Thanks for teaching me that we are all God's children.

To all the relatives and friends of the beautiful people who lost their lives in the senseless Orlando, Florida shooting, God made us all uniquely different. The law gives us a right to choose our own walk in life. It is a freedom that is suppose to serve all of mankind. When people use a person's way of life to commit hate crimes, it demonstrates the inhumanity in that individual who is truly submerged in prejudice, and thus they declare themselves to be right. We are all God's children, and if we remember that, we will so easily recognize that we are all brother's and sister' of the same Father. I pray a sweet peace for all of those who lost their lives and a comfort to the families that lost them. The memory lives on!

Contents

"A Gay Affair"

PRELUDE

When I was a kid, about nine or ten, I think, my dad told me to 'always be a man.' No matter what it was, he would say, "Boy, be a man!" He told me that being a man was the best thing that you could ever be. "Well, next to God," he would smile and add. My father grew up in a period in which it was totally taboo to be gay, or even to be known as a sissy, which back in the day meant that you were soft and not all boy. So, every now and again, he would also say, "And don't be no sissy!" And whenever he said that, I stuck my chest out and tried to look tough.

My dad was a hard core ex-Marine. He never talked much about the war, but he just seemed to be angry about everything, especially gays and lesbians. Whenever he saw one, male or female, if I looked toward them, he would slap me really hard and say, "Don't look at that thing. You'll turn to stone!" And I'd quickly turn my head off in another direction. Out of the corner of my eye, I'd often catch him looking at me to see if I was crying or not; but I never cried. I just wondered why he hated gays so much. So, when he found out that his eleven-year old nephew was gay, my first cousin Tony, I thought he was going to blow up the world.

You see, over their entire lives, Tony's dad and my dad had always been very close brothers. My dad always told me how he and his brother, my uncle Anthony, did everything together; they even joined the Marines together, married two sisters from the same house, and were best friends. So when everyone found out that little Tony didn't want to be "a boy" anymore, his dad and mine took it really hard. They must have tried everything they could think of in their quest to make him be what they felt he should be, or, as my dad would say, "A man." From the age of eleven through eighteen, Uncle Anthony must have made little Tony attend every karate class in the city. He and my dad thought that this would make him tough. Before his first karate class, Uncle Anthony forced Tony to join my brother Sally's wrestling team, which was a bad idea because Tony always let the other guy pin him down. My dad favored Sal, as we called him, much more than me because Sal did whatever dad wanted him to do, and was always good at it, no matter what it was – football, baseball, soccer, basketball, wrestling, karate. . .

Of all the sports, karate was my favorite; I was pretty good at it. I played a little football, but I was too short to participate in any of the other sports. My dad never liked the idea that my mom named my brother Sally, but it was her grandfather's name, and he had given them ten acres of land to build our house on.

I remember one day when we were out in the back yard playing, and Puggley, one of our friends from down the road, came over. We were all around the same age, except Tony's big brother, Antoine, who was a couple of years older than us; but we all hung out together. On this particular day when we were about fourteen years old, Sal threw the football to Tony, and, instead of catching it, Tony turned his back and covered his head. Puggley walked over, picked up the football, looked at Tony, and said, "Your name

2

should have been Sally because you act like a big girl!" Tony turned to Puggley, snapped his fingers at him, and said, "I'm not big or fat like you"; and then walked toward him and said, "If you call me a girl again, I'm gonna kick you in your fat butt!" Now, Puggley was about 5 foot 5 inches and 170 pounds; he was a big boy in comparison to Tony's slender 5 foot 90 pounds. Puggley had only been in the community for about a year, and his parents were very strict. Although we went to school together, he hardly ever came outside after school; and that day may have been one of those days that he wished he had stayed in because he walked over to Tony, balled his fist, and was going to say something – but he never got it out. In one swift motion, Tony reached out, grabbed Puggley's arm, and tossed him to the ground. Puggley sat there for a second, and then jumped up; but, before he could catch his balance, Tony flipped him to the ground again. This time, when Puggley got up, he tried to rush Tony and tackle him to the ground; but, once again, Tony, being as good in karate as he was, just side-stepped him and gave him a wedgey as he passed by. Puggley was so upset that he left and went home with his pants still wedged in his butt.

After that, Puggley never called Tony anything, but Tony – well, at least not loud enough for Tony to hear him. We were cousins and best friends.

CHAPTER 1

Coming of Age

When we came of age, we all joined the U.S. Marines, one by one: Antoine first, then Sal, and then Puggley and I joined together. However, Tony wasn't having any of it. Right after school, he went to Rio and become a clothing designer. No one heard from him in the first year, but then I got a letter from my mom saying that he had actually became a very successful clothing designer and was making a ton of money. Mom said that he was making so much money that my dad and uncle Anthony had learned to accept him for who he was, or "for the good gifts that he was always sending," mom added.

When I was in my second year of Marine Corps service, I was in interrogation training – a class that Antoine had recommended that all of us take. The main program was called Initiate, Interrogate, and Eradicate (I.I.E. was its code name), but I had no idea what that meant; I just knew that if I completed the class, I would then be in the same unit as my brother Sal and Antoine. I didn't find out until we were at graduation that the government had been creating an elite team of Marines to fight the drug war in third world countries that were trafficking drugs to the U.S. It didn't really matter to me because, by the time I found out, I was gung-ho and excited about being in the same unit as my brother, my cousin, and my best friend Puggley. Nothing else mattered; it was like old times again back home in the streets, walking down the country roads. The only difference was that we were strapped, loaded to bear whatever, or deal with whatever might jump out at us. I never really got excited because it was all just a bunch of training missions. I mean, we were on base at Camp Lejeune, N.C.! What could happen there? The most they could do was scare the hell out of me. They couldn't hurt me or kill me; so, "What the hell," I thought.

One day, as we were walking on a wooded trail, I heard the sound of someone walking. I alerted the team leader, Puggley at the time. [You see, they rotated us every day for proficiency, and a test of courage and strength, to challenge our leadership skills and our ability to command.] And on this particular day, the sun was shining bright, birds were chirping, and Puggley gave the sign to stop. He looked around, and then gave the sign to move out. As we started to proceed, he signaled me to move to the front and take the point. That was fine with me because, even though it was training, it didn't matter if it was real or not because I had shot the highest score on the rifle and pistol range; so, if something were to jump out, his ass would be mine.

Now, as a Marine, I had learned the hard way that the enemy doesn't always jump out at you, but sometimes jumps down on you. All of our guns had only blanks. Therefore, "What the hell is going on?" I thought, as someone jumped out of a tree onto my back. The force was so heavy that it knocked me straight to the ground, my rifle flew out of my hands, and I felt a sting in my right shoulder as if something had bit me, and, suddenly, everything started to go black. I could hear people talking, but I couldn't understand what they were saying. They had covered my head with a sack; my body felt numb, and I could hardly move, but I could hear someone saying, "I hate you f--k--g Americans." It sounded like a Latin accent, but I couldn't be sure because someone then said, "Kill all these assholes!" and his accent sounded either African or Jamaican. I went to lift my arms and realized that they were bound along with my feet. I could hear Puggley say, "Get off of me, motherf r!" Then, I heard the sound of a hammer being cocked on a gun, and, in a Middle Eastern or African voice, I heard him say to Puggley, "Say good-bye, American piece of shit!" And then, Bang! Bang! Two shots rang out. I wanted to scream out, "Puggley!" but my training had taught me not to. I then heard another person say, "Drag that piece of shit out of here, Hiyako, Hiyako!" I had heard those words before: it was oriental – Japanese, I thought. I remembered hearing them in the movie "The Last Samurai." So, then I was wondering how many people could there be. I knew that everything that I'd learned in the last two years would have to be applied, but I was somewhat dazed – wondering how something like this could happen on a Marine Corps base.

I must have passed out for a moment because my eyes were open, but I couldn't see a thing. Before, I could see daylight from the bottom of the sack that they had tied around my neck, but not this time; it was total darkness, so I assumed that some time had passed, and that it was night. I no longer wanted to play dead; I wanted to know what the hell was going on, who was holding me hostage, and how the hell was I going to get out of there. I pulled all my thoughts together, and remembered an incident, when I was ten years old, in which my dad had taken off his belt – preparing to tan my hide for stealing and racing his farm tractor. I had pretended that I couldn't breathe, and had made myself choke. It had worked for him, so maybe it would work here, I thought. I made every choking noise that a person choking could possibly make, and then just lay still as if I had passed out. Then I heard one say in plain old American English, "Get that bag off his head; he's no good to us dead." As he raced to get the bag off my head, I began to hold my breath so that I would look the part of a man choking. As soon as he ripped the bag off, he began to question me. "What are the government's plans? Are you a part of some secret government operation here in the U.S.?" As soon as he said those things, I knew that this was just another part of the training mission. I was still a little drowsy, but I managed to give him a smile. "You are being trained to stop us, aren't you? Answer me!" he said, and then slapped me really hard in the face. I almost pissed my pants, and thought to myself, "This shit might be real." I tried to sit up and he kicked me straight in the gut. He kicked so hard that I passed gas, and boy, did it hurt! While I was laying there on the floor, I heard one laugh and say, "Man, you really kicked the shit out of him," as he fanned his hand and the other two laughed.

My mind first went to Marine Corps training ("name, rank, and serial number"), but, then I thought, "This could mean my life. I mean, I already heard him shoot Puggley." So, I had to come up with something quick, and I yelled out, "I never wanted to be a part of this bullshit anyway. Cut my hands loose and I'll tell you anything you want to know." "I'm not untying anything, asshole, and you will answer all of my questions!" Wham! went another slap upside my head, and he added, "You will tell me or I'll put two in you like I did your buddy's!" When he said that, my fear turned into pure anger – thinking that he likely was the one who had killed Puggley, and maybe Sal, too, because he was in flank, right behind Puggley. I lifted my head and tried to focus my eyes on the dimly lit room. As I turned my head, I could see about five other people in the room. When I looked to my left, he slapped me again, this time right in the mouth, busting my lip. Blood flew everywhere. "What are looking around for? You don't have but one thing to do, and that is to answer my questions." I looked down at my feet; the drug that they had given me was starting to wear off, and my vision was starting to clear up some. The drug, whatever it was, made me feel heavy, as if I was bound to the floor. But, when my vision cleared all the way, I could see that I was not bound to the floor, but my hands were cuffed together with plastic police handcuffs. My head was starting to clear, and I remembered that in the classroom we had been taught to stretch the cuffs as far apart as possible, and then bring our hands together quickly and pull them out. The class had taught me well, and the timing was perfect. "Hey, Ron, look at this," one of them said. As soon as he turned his head, I was out of the cuffs and on his ass like stink on shit. I locked my left arm around his neck, wrapped both of my legs around his, and pulled his pistol from out of his waistband. I then took five quick kill shots, which dropped all five of them simultaneously; but I pistol whipped Ron with three good whacks across his face, took one step backward, and put one bullet in his head at close range. I was looking for his brains to be scattered all over the floor; instead, there was just a little red dot that, up close, didn't even look like blood. As I stooped down to take a closer look, one of the other guys began to get up. I hurriedly put one more in him; then, the other three began to get up, so, this time, I aimed for the face. "No!" one of them shouted out, "not in the face." "Yeah, that shit hurts," said the one on the end. "Tell me about it," said Ron, now getting to his feet as the lights came on bright. "I thought they said that we wouldn't get shot in the face," said one of the other four. "Quit your crying, ya big baby. I just took one to the head," said Ron, getting to his feet. "What the hell is going on here?" I asked, backing away from all of them. One by one they began to rip off their faces; well, not quite. Actually, they were ripping off false faces, and the second face revealed to me was that of my own brother, Sal. "Alright somebody, tell me what the f--k is going on!" "Relax Little Brother. You did good." "Good!" I shouted angrily, with some blood still trickling down the side of my busted lip. "Come here, little brother; let me help you clean. . ." "Help me? Why didn't you help me just now when I was laying down there on the floor?" I asked, cutting short his brotherly gesture. "It's part of your training, Marine," said Ron, now revealing himself as Major Ron Travis, U.S.M.C. / C.I.A. detachment commander. I immediately snapped to attention. "At ease, son; and be proud of yourself," he said. "It's not every Marine who can say that he successfully pistol whipped his unit commander." "Sorry, sir. I thought that it was. . ." as he cut me off, saying, "Real. It gets a lot more real than this because the guys that we are going to be up against are a lot more intense and most likely will only ask you once. That is why it is imperative that this team remain elusive and avoid capture at all cost. If you do get captured, you'll be on your own; otherwise, their interrogation teams will make you wish that you had never been born." "I was beginning to feel like that a few moments ago," I said. "Good," he added. "That lets me know I'm doing my job," he said, putting his mask back on while leaving the room.

By now, Sal had made his way over to me with a wash rag in his hand. He looked at me real seriously and then burst out laughing. I looked back at him and asked, "What the hell's so funny?" "When the Major kicked you in your gut, did you fart? Or did you shit on yourself? 'Cause, bro, you sure were stinking!" "Yeah, whatever man," I said as I began to clean up my face. Wiping the blood off my lip, and the effects of the slaps to my face continued to really hurt! "Come here, Sam. You want to see something?" he said as he led me by the arm to the window where the rest of the team was. I could see Puggley lying on the floor. "Turn the sound up," said one of the guys, laughing. Then he walked over to me, shook hands, and introduced himself. "I'm John Johnson, but everybody calls me J.J. You want to know why?" he asked. "Well, that's easy enough," I said. "Because your name is John Johnson." "Boom!" He said super loudly, startling the heck out of me, and adding, "Wrong! They call me J.J. because I'm like that dude Kid Dynamite!!! You get it? You remember that show from the 70's, Good something it was called; you remember the little guy who came out and shouted 'Kid Dynamite!?'" "Yeah, I remember the show," I said. "Well, that's me. I'm the demo expert, and any kind of explosive you want, I can build it or dismantle it," he said.

After that brief conversation, I walked over and stood beside Sal and another member of the team, who introduced himself as Stoney. He didn't have much to say, nor did the other member of the team who did not introduce himself. They all stood at the two-way mirror, watching the other team interrogate Puggley. "Turn it up," Stoney said. "Your boy's crying like a baby," he said, talking about Puggley. As I looked through the window, I could see the Major standing over Puggley and doing to him just as he had done to me. The only difference was that – while Puggley had been out cold, they stuck two plastic head thumb tacks into his lower back and through his clothing, so that every time he moved it caused him pain. This was truly a learning experience for me because Puggley actually thought he had been shot. It was a mind game: One stood behind him and, every now and then, pushed in on the tacks; furthermore, they had poured fake blood onto the part of the floor where he laid, and had also saturated his lower shirt and pants. "You gonna die, asshole, unless you tell me what I want to know," Major Travis said. "Let him die; he's going to bleed to death anyway," the other member said. Then a third person said, "Let me put one in his head. We already have enough Intel that we got from the others." "Yeah, but this one's the leader, and he has a lot more Intel than the rest of them," said Major Travis. I felt so sorry for Puggley because Stoney and the other guy were betting that he would crack. Sal looked at me and, as we listened to them put him through hell; the Major put his boot to the side of Puggley's head and said, "I'm tired of f--king with you." By now we could hear Puggley sniffling and starting to shake and mumble. "He's going to crack any minute," Stoney said, and added, "it's like money in the bank." That's when Sal said to Stoney, "I bet a hundred dollars he don't crack," and the other guy said, "I'll take fifty of that." Sal looked at me and winked, and I winked back and smiled to myself because, at the moment Puggley started to shake, I knew what was coming next. (Having grown up with Puggley, we knew that whenever his body shook, he was really mad. It was a nervous condition, and, once he started to shake, we knew that we had best get out of his way!) I watched one of the interrogators stand back off of him; even though he had on a mask, I could tell by his body movements that he was my cousin Antoine. Until then, Puggley hadn't said a thing. "You just as well talk; the rest of your friends are dead," said the Major, stepping on Puggley's chest. "Well you best better kill me, too, motherf----r!" "You best better kill me, too, motherf !" said Puggley again, as he somehow got to his feet. Puggley broke the plastic cuff and started to rip the sack off his head. The Major and the other team members tried to subdue him, but, at this point, Puggley wasn't having any of that! I mean, I thought that he was going to kill the Major. He slapped Puggley with the pistol a couple of times, but Puggley had the Major in a choke hold and wasn't about to let go. They were beating the hell out of him, but Puggley would not yield. Finally, Antoine walked up to him and hit him in the head with his pistol. Big Puggley went down like a rock sinking in water.

I stood at the window and watched them pull Puggley off the Major's chest, and begin to revive the Major. Sal collected his money from Stoney and the other team member. The five of us walked outside to head back to the barracks to get cleaned up. "What's going to happen to Puggley?" I asked. "The same thing that happened to you: Nothing! It's a training class," said Sal. "But don't think about going out tonight because there's still more fun to come in the morning," he added.

I had been in the barracks for about forty-five minutes when I looked out and saw Puggley coming up the sidewalk. At first I was going to wait; but then I changed my mind and decided to just go take a shower and hit the sack, and get ready for tomorrow.

The nights were short and mostly sleepless, especially after a day like that day. It was three o'clock in the morning, I couldn't sleep, and I just laid there wondering, "What the hell am I doing here? If this is training, what the hell will it be like when we get out there for the real deal?" Puggley must have been wondering the same because, every now and again, I heard him bump up against the wall. Then, I fell into a deep sleep for a brief moment just before sunrise. Then, Bam! Bam! Bam! "Wake up, wake up, wake up, wake up, Sam!" shouted Sal, knocking on my room door. My eyelids were heavy as if they had been glued shut, and my body ached all over; so, I decided to lay there for a few minutes more. I must have fallen back to sleep, because – when I opened my eyes again – the sun was up and very bright. "Oh shit!" I said. As I jumped out of bed, I looked at the clock, which read 9:15am. "Damn! I'm going to be late for class," I thought to myself. But then Puggley knocked one time and opened the door. "Hey Sam! Are you going eat? And why did they let us sleep late?" he asked all in one breath. "Because you guys got pretty beat up yesterday," said Sal, walking into my room. "But both of you did good. The Major was impressed, and it takes a hell of lot to impress that SOB."

"Which SOB would that be?" the Major asked, as he walked into the room. "Attention!" Sal shouted. As the Major entered, he looked at Sal and smiled, and then said, "At ease, gentlemen." He walked around my bed and looked at the picture of my girl on the wall, and said "You men get some breakfast and report to the ready room at 11:00 am." "Yes, sir!" we all responded. Then, as casually as he had walked in, he walked back out. "Man, that was close!" said Sal, wiping the sweat off his forehead. Puggley and I looked at one another, and started laughing. "Yeah, that's what you get," said Puggley. "Oh, you guys think that's funny?" Sal asked. "Yeah. I think so – especially after that trick that y'all pulled on us yesterday," I said as I headed into the bathroom to brush my teeth.

When I came out of the bathroom, it was clear that both of them had left for breakfast. I was glad that they had gone before me because, every morning, I liked to say a prayer before I started my day. Once that was done, I dressed and hurried to breakfast.

The mess hall was like any other Marine Corps mess hall except that they kept us separated from the rest of the units. We had our own little section next to the officers' section. I thought that was pretty cool because the cooks gave us the same treatment as they gave the officers. Sal said that they gave us that space in case we wanted to talk about different things that had happened within our unit. I then said to Sal that I had no idea just how top secret our training classes were because, when I told someone about our unit, they said that they had never heard of it before. "Now you know to keep your mouth shut!" said Antoine, walking over and wearing captain bars. Sal immediately called the table to attention. The three of us stood up and locked heels – me, Sal, and Puggley; but everyone else just sat there. And J.J. was making jokes, saying, "Boy, we are going to blow something up today!" Antoine then looked at Sal and started laughing, saying, "Leave them guys alone, man!" Sal smiled, sat down, and said, "You never salute any officers in your unit. Get in the practice of not doing that. You'll find out why when we get into class today; but remember that that is just for the officers in our unit." I hunched Sal and asked, "Is he really a captain?" "Yeah," replied Sal. "We all get field grade promotions once we complete training school. Hell, I'm slated to become a first lieutenant; Stoney, J.J., and Sparky are all captains now. I'll get mine officially after my next mission is completed," said Sal, looking up as the Major walked in. As Antoine had instructed, no one got up or called anyone to attention. The Major sat down with us and asked, "You boys ready to have some fun today?" He smiled at Puggley, and then added, "Andy, you have a visitor at the front gate. You know the policy: You have to meet

13

them off post; just be back by 1600 today." "Will do, Major," responded Antoine as he got up.

Antoine had always been a private guy; outside of sports, he had never hung with anyone else. So, to hear that he had a visitor was really creepy. He slapped a high five with Sal and left. "Who do you think came to see him?" I asked Sal. "Oh, he will tell you if he wants you to know," responded Sal, and then added, "We reserve the right to keep all our visitors private – well, at least between us; but there is no privacy to the C.I.A., C.I.D., N.S.A., and, of course, I.I.E. These agencies have access to our whereabouts at all times."

After we finished eating, Puggley and I reported to the weaponry and self-defense class. To me, this was going to be the best part of the training program because I could take out my frustrations on the instructors and be praised for it. I was about to walk into the weaponry class when something, or rather someone, caught my eye; and man, was she ever an eye-catcher! She was Asian, about five feet six, with the most beautiful complexion I had ever seen. "Who is that?" I asked one of the guys entering the self-defense class. "That's the new assistant instructor." "I hear that she's pretty good," he added. "Pretty girl, nice body, and can fight, too! Man, you know that that's my type of girl!" I said, looking at Puggley. "Come on, Sam! You know that we are supposed to be going to weaponry class first," said Puggley. "That's not what the Major said, Puggley. What he said was for us to report to weaponry and self-defense, and he didn't say in what order," I said as I started to walk into her class.

Then Antoine called Puggley and me to come into the weaponry class. When we walked in, I was amazed at all the toys and gadgets they had that were lethal weapons, but, more than that, I was curious to know who had come to visit Antoine! Antoine knew that

I wanted to ask him, so he just came out and said, "I know you boots want to know who came out to see me," and at that moment he picked up one of the mini submachine guns and started explaining its functions. I said, "Wait a minute, man. I thought that you were going to tell us who came out. You know that we are family. Is anybody sick or anything?" I asked. "No, Sam," he finally responded. "It was Tony. He's down here for the weekend – him and a few of his friends. I wasn't going to tell you guys because he felt that you wouldn't want to hang out with him and his gay friends, especially you, Puggley." "Yeah, you got that right," said Puggley. "Come on, man! It's Tony! It will be fun – like old times. We all will be hanging out together," I said, trying to persuade Puggley. "Cut the crap, Sam. You know damn well I never hung out with Tony!" said Puggley. "Besides, I'm not going to no gay bar." "You guys are not going to a gay bar, are you?" I asked, with a little hesitancy. Antoine looked at me and said, "Tony is my brother. I'm going wherever he wants me to. You guys don't have to," he added. However, by the end of the day, I had talked Puggley into coming along with Antoine, Sal, and me. All the way there, Puggley bitched and repeated, "I'm not going inside no gay bar. I'll wait outside here in the car." When we pulled up, it wasn't a gay bar at all, but a family restaurant.

Tony hadn't got much bigger, but his wild outfits had gotten much more feminine and flamboyant. He was dressed like a gay version of Steve Harvey, with a pink vest loaded with sparkles. The car he was driving was a brand new hot pink Bogotti. It was nothing for Sal and me to walk up to Tony and give him a hug. After all, we were all family, and there was no law or side look when you were hugging family. We exchanged greetings and made wise cracks to one another. The whole time that the three of us were talking, Antoine and Puggley were standing to the side. "Hey Puggley," said Tony. "What's up?" responded Puggley. Then the two looked each other in the eye for a second, and Tony said, "I hope you guys are hungry, because we have that table over there to the far right." He pointed to it as we walked in. It looked like a thanksgiving table, or a banquet fit for a king; and, at that table were three of the most beautiful women that I had ever seen in my life. When Tony introduced us, Sal started stuttering, Puggley started drooling, and I don't know what the hell Antoine was doing because, by the time he got to April, I automatically forgot every other name and person that I had spoken with all day.

The evening went great, the food and wine were excellent, and April was the icing on the cake. She was one of Tony's clothing models. "Well educated, speaks with great intelligence, and makes nice money, too! Hell, I think I'm in love!" I thought for a moment – until Puggley bumped me and said, "Man, will you move down so somebody else can sit beside you?" That's pretty much how the night went. It was almost like old times. Tony had always had a group of pretty girls in his corner, which I could never figure out. I mean, most gay guys seemed to have a gang of pretty girlfriends.

The night was going fine until Tony accidentally touched Puggley's hand while he was laughing. Puggley looked a Tony and said, "Don't touch my hand again. You know that I don't play that shit." I looked at Puggley and said, "Lighten up, man! It's just Tony." "Yeah, that's what I know," said Puggley, sighing. "He must want another wedgy," said Sal, laughing. All of us laughed together except Puggley. "Y'all think that shit is funny," said Puggley, smiling; he then added, "That was a long time ago." "Not that long ago," Tony mumbled under his breath. "More wine?" the waiter asked, interrupting any response that Puggley could give. He made his way around the table and finally got to Tony, when he stooped, gave him a hug, and asked if everything was to his satisfaction. "Everything is fabulous," replied Tony, and then

16

added, "Let me introduce you to some of my family." Just as he was about to introduce Sal as his cousin, Antoine got up and went to the restroom. Tony introduced the waiter as Parris, and Sal and I shook hands with him, but Puggley gave him a raised fist. Parris told us that he was the owner; there was no secret that he was gay, and, as I looked around, I noticed that there was only one other family within the restaurant; everyone else was paired up – two men at this table, two women at that table, two women sitting at the bar, two men way down on the other end of the bar, etc. It was clear that this was a gay restaurant, the first I'd ever seen; but I was distracted by April's beauty and the expensive wine. And, as I looked at Puggley, I could see that he was coming to the same conclusion. I exchanged phone numbers with April, who, a few moments before, had indicated that she didn't do it on the first date. In addition, I knew that we had an early next day, not to mention the fact that I really didn't want anyone to see me coming out of a gay restaurant.

I hurried to the back of the restaurant to the restroom to tell Antoine that we were ready to go, but he was not there; so, I returned to the table and asked, "Did he come back here?" "No," said Sal, standing up. As we were about to leave the table, a gay waiter came over and asked for Sal. Puggley and I both pointed to Sal. The young man gave him Antoine's car keys and said, "The gentleman asked me to give you his keys. He left with a young lady." Upon hearing that, I remembered a lady who had been sitting at the center of the bar – pretty, at least from a distance. "That lucky dog," I thought to myself; but that thought was interrupted when I looked around and realized how crowded it had suddenly gotten. "Where did all these people come from?" Sal asked Tony. "It's gay, and it's happy hour – buy one, get one free." "Okay," replied Tony. We gave Tony a hug, and Puggley gave him another raised fist as he walked past and said, "Later."

17

CHAPTER 2
Things are not What they Seem

The morning came with a slight hangover, but I was up and ready for the next challenge. We all were at the mess hall having breakfast except for Antoine, J.J., and Stoney. I asked the wire man, or Sparky as we called him, about their absence, but he just said, "The Major will brief you on it." And just as he said that, the Major walked in and began to brief us on our comrades, although our adversaries were having a meeting of their own.

"Is everything in place? Because, when this meeting is over, only two mother f s walk away from the table. You got that? Those f--king pigs die at the table. So, pay close attention to what I'm saying and don't f--k this up. The first toast will be to our new alliance, but the second will be to say goodbye to old fools. He's my father, but his way of doing business is as soft and backward as his gay and lesbian friends. I will make the deal with his new U.S. contacts myself. It's a new day," said Pocco, warning his most trustworthy friend. Pocco was the son of the man who had become number one on the hit list of over twenty different countries world-wide. His ruthless international drug dealings, gun running, and trail of murders (including seven U.S. federal agents and dozens of law enforcement officers from different agencies around the world) had made him the number one reason why I.I.E. was created. His father was a clever, but careless, cold-hearted murderer. The person Pocco was giving instructions to was his childhood best friend and first cousin, Paul. The two men discussed the details of killing Pocco's father.

Pocco was the thirty-two year old son of Freddie Federico Alveras, the murderous fugitive who had eluded law enforcement agencies for over twenty years. Freddie, as he liked to call himself, had become so powerful that no other mob – Chinese, Italian, or whatever – would ever get close to him and his dealings. His murders appeared to have been done by ghosts. Also, he was famous for his cross dressing and his female impersonations; for years, no one knew his name, race, or even his sex, for that matter. His elusive ways had also earned him the nickname "Chameleon."

As his son and nephew sat there plotting his demise, the doors opened as Freddie walked in, wearing a milk white two thousand dollar Armanie suit, black shirt, purple vest, and pink tie. With his female impersonators draped on both arms, he strolled into the large dining room, accompanied also by two new American contacts and two gay bodyguards, who closed the door behind them. The bodyguards were armed with Uzis (fully automatic submachine guns) holstered in hot pink holsters. "Father, you're early. Everything is not quite ready yet," said Pocco, jumping to his feet. "What do you mean?" asked Freddie, smiling. "The food is on the table, our new American contacts are here, you are here, and my favorite nephew is here." "Yes, father. But the wine is not on the table yet, and where is Uncle Jose and your regular bodyguards?" "Those two lovely creatures have come all the way from America, from a city called Baltimore; they have come to learn how we do business here, and to learn how important it is to follow instructions." Then he added, "But as for your uncle, my dear brother, well, he's getting old, and he says that these dining room chairs are too hard to sit on.

But, as for me, I like sitting on hard things." He then smiled at the two female impersonators, who pulled his seat back and waited for him to sit; but, instead, he walked over and sat where his brother normally sat and said "Oooh. It is a hard seat!" Pocco turned his head away from his father in disgust and shame. Then, he looked at

19

his cousin Paul, knowing that his plans had been disrupted by the changing of the guards and his father's early arrival; so he decided to wait for another time to plot it out again. All of them then sat down, admiring the banquet style table, which resembled an all-you-can-eat buffet.

Everything was there except for the wine, and everyone present knew that no wine on the table meant that Freddie likely would get very upset. "How do you know if you can trust those two?" asked Pocco, trying to show concern, as if he cared about his father's safety – then adding, "I haven't even questioned them yet to test their loyalty, father. You are getting. . ." "What?" asked Freddie, cutting him off. "Soft?" "No, father. That's not what I was about to say," responded Pocco. "I was going to say. . ." "Slow," said Freddie, interrupting him again. "You see, Mr. Jones, my son worries about the things that he has no need to worry about." Buttering his bread with his butter knife, he began to explain, "You see how softly the butter glides onto the bread? It's because it's soft. So, you see, Pocco, sometimes softer is better." Then, leaning over to his son, he added, "Hard is only good when it needs to be." And, with that said, he briefly looked Pocco in the eyes and, in one clean stroke, slashed his throat from ear to ear. His nephew Paul clapped his hands twice, the guards opened the door, and the gay server brought in the wine. And, as Pocco sat at the table bleeding to death, Freddie looked at him and asked, "Was that hard enough for you? I told you that all of you were here to learn about loyalty and how we do things over here and around the world, especially to traitors. There's no rule on punishment or who gets punished." He then added, "I told you, son, the only mistake I ever made was to marry your mother and pretend to like being with her – or with any other woman, for that matter. I wanted to be free. The moment that I discovered it was Steve I was meant for, not Eve." As Pocco gasped his last breath, Freddie barked out, "Let's eat!" As he gazed about the table, Freddie then asked the American, "This little distraction is not going to ruin your dinner, is it?" The American looked at his partner, who had already started eating, and then, with a smile, said, "No. Not at all," as he cut into his medium rare steak and began to eat, too. His face showing no emotion, Freddie stopped eating, raised his glass, and said, "A toast to our new partnership!" He then looked at his nephew Paul and asked, "Is there anything else that we should be toasting to?" "Honor, Uncle," came the reply. "Yes, nephew. Honor! Let us toast to honor and loyalty, for these are things that we must have in an organization such as ours."

The meeting lasted for three hours – maybe more – with Pocco's dead, bloody body sitting there throughout. They then devised a plan that would allow his army of drug lords to infiltrate the U.S. "legally" – with absolutely no suspicion, and, once in the U.S., set up legitimate businesses with an inside, under-the-table trade in drugs, guns, and military top secrets. "We understand that your government is in early stages of developing a land microscopic spy and defense security system," said Freddie, then adding, "I understand that you can post it thirty feet in the air and attach it to anything." "It's your eyes in the dark," said the American, taking another sip of wine and quickly adding, "But that's a long ways away; however, I'm impressed that you have knowledge about such top secret material." "But, nevertheless," said Freddie, interrupting, "let us discuss our plan of operation. The first group will land in Miami, the second will set up in L.A., but our main club will be in Baltimore, Maryland – where my two newest bodyguards are from. These are the most popular cities that perform same-sex marriages. Where are my manners? Allow me to introduce them to you," said Freddie, speaking of the guards at the door. "In red is Dominic, and in hot pink is Marcella. They will be my eyes and ears as we move forward." He then began to explain his devious plot to set up shop right underneath the noses of the very ones who were in pursuit of him. "Dominic and Marcella will handle all the business from our office in Baltimore. We will open up a same-sex marriage club that will recruit only college students who are drug-free. All members must be gay and loyal to the club. They all will be exceedingly skilled in self-defense – with NO exceptions! Also, we will train them to be marksmen and weapons experts in all fields, and then we will recruit non-club members from abroad to marry our men. These overseas people will be club members who are currently handling our affairs in other countries; most of them are gay like myself, but some are not. I don't like heterosexuals – they can't be trusted!" "Too much testosterone," he added as he walked out, smiling as he passed by and looked at his dead son.

Three months passed, and the I.I.E. team had just about finished its training; they were now trusted enough to go out on the town unsupervised. It was Friday and liberty had just been sounded; but, in this unit, everything was a mission. Before the team could do anything, they had to be briefed. So, at 1500 hours, the Major walked into the briefing room and laid down the law to all of the new team members. "I just want to make certain that you guys don't get yourselves involved in any fights or foolishness that would draw attention to you or the uniform that you're wearing." I quickly raised my hand. "Yeah, Sam. What is it?" asked the Major. "Does that mean that we have to wear our uniforms?" I asked. "No, not literally; but whenever and wherever you go, you will always be Marines, and you will conduct yourself as such. However, if you should find yourself in some sort of mishap, then contact me, not your primary unit commander, or anyone else who is not directly involved in this unit. And, from your training, you know not to talk to anyone other than me. Obey the laws of the land, and render yourselves to be submissive to any law enforcement agency to answer name rank and serial number only; stay focused and enjoy your liberty. Remember to take and keep your phone on all the time, because, in this unit, you are on call 24/7." As soon as he finished briefing us, Sal came in and stood by the door. "And one last thing," the Major added. "What's that, Sir?" Puggley asked. "Stop and see the nurse on your way off base. And that's an order!" said the Major, as he walked away.

Simultaneously, Antoine walked in. "What's up, boots?" He asked, smiling at us. "Yo! You still riding up to B-More tonight, right?" I asked. "Yeah, Sam. You boots can ride with me," said Antoine. "Where's Sal? Is he coming with us?" I asked. "Nah. Sal is on his first mission," he said. "And don't ask me about it because I don't know about it, and I wouldn't tell you two boots about it even if I did," he added. But it was cool because I knew that Antoine would have firsthand info on whatever Sal was doing because he was our second-in-command. This was my chance to see if all that crap about the 'code of silence' that they were teaching us really meant something to Antoine, because, when we were little boys, he always bragged about everything he did, especially after he had had a drink or two. "Of course you know that you boots are going to pay for the gas," he added. "And hurry up! I only have a thirty-six-hour pass; you guys have two weeks to play!" With that said, the two of us rushed back to our barrack and packed up. I didn't know what to pack. All I knew was that I hadn't been home in about nine months, and that I had pretty much cut all ties before I left. Puggley still had his girl, Pam. He often showed me pictures of her and one of her girlfriends, Angie, who was super fine. But Angie had two kids and had just turned twenty-one.

On the way to Baltimore, we talked about everything except us. We talked about events when we were young, our old girlfriends, our summer trips to the country with our dads, and how we had shot Mr. John's bull in the butt with the BB rifle and had run across the field in front of him. It was crazy; the bull would first take off in one direction, and then, after seeing us, he would make a 360 degree turn, and come charging behind us. Fortunately, we always beat him to the other side. "Man, that used to be a lot of fun," I said. "No, fool. That was crazy!" said Puggley. "I will never go down there with you guys ever again; that was crazy!" said Puggley again. Then, he further added, "You guys never told me that the bull was going to turn around and come after us." "We told you to run," I reminded him. "But, no. You yelled out, 'Man, you guys are a bunch of pussies.'" "Yeah, then I turned around, and saw that damn bull running up on me," said Puggley, as he took a deep breath, adding, "That was some crazy shit, man; I could have been killed." I looked at Antoine and he looked at me, and we both burst out laughing! "What?" said Puggley.

"You guys thought that shit was funny!? "Yeah. That's the fastest I ever saw your little fat ass run," said Antoine, laughing. "That's alright," replied Puggley. "At least I had the balls to run. Your faggy ass brother Tony wouldn't even leave the fence." Antoine hit the brakes and pulled over rapidly, weaving through traffic, then coming to a screeching halt. "What the f--k did you say about my brother?" asked Antoine, jumping out of the car. "Motherf----r, don't you ever talk about my little brother," said Antoine, opening the back door. I quickly jumped out and got between them.

"Hey, come on, Antoine. He didn't mean no harm. It's just Puggley being the asshole that he is," I said. "Yeah, man. What's up with that, Antoine? Why you all wound up?" asked Puggley. "Just keep my little brother's name out of your mouth," replied Antoine, getting back into the car. Then, just as he put the car in drive to pull off, a police car pulled up behind us. Two officers got out. One walked up to the left side, and the other to the right – each with a flashlight in one hand and the other hand resting on their weapon. They walked up to the car and said sternly, "Keep your hands where we can see them!" The officer on the left then said, "I need to see your driver's license, registration, and insurance card." "Is something wrong, officer? We just pulled over to check the air in the rear tire," said Antoine, as he handed him his military ID. "Captain, U.S.M.C.," said the police officer. "Oh, my fault, sir," said Antoine as he next handed him his driver's license. "You guys be on your way," said the officer, winking as he looked at his partner and said, "These guys are alright." Then, he asked Antoine, "Everything is alright, isn't it?" "Yes, officer. Everything is fine." "I don't know Jack," said the other officer, adding, "When we came across the overpass, it looked as if you were about to be in an altercation with the gentleman in the back seat, and this guy" (pointing at me) "was coming in between the two of you." "No, officer. Our friend in the back was just getting a little car sick, so we were checking on him as we were looking at the rear tire." "Oh yeah?" said the officer as he looked in the back at Puggley, and asked "Are you alright?" "Yeah. I'm alright," responded Puggley, saying further, "I think it might be the steak I had for dinner. The waiter said that the meat came from the bull, so it tasted a little different from the other meat." "Yeah, officer. He's full of bull, if you know what I mean," said Antoine to the officer standing at his window. The officer smiled and said, "You guys be careful, and have a safe trip." We thanked him, and Antoine pulled off. From that stop on, the ride was pretty quiet until we got to Baltimore.

I was half asleep when I heard Antoine say, "Welcome to Baltimore," reading the sign on Route 295. I could also hear Puggley in the back seat talking to someone on the phone. Antoine took the Monroe Street exit, and pulled into the Royal Farms store "You boots want some coffee? He asked, as he got out. "No," replied Puggley, then adding, "You can just pop the trunk for me so I can get my stuff; my girl is right over there." But, instead, Antoine kept walking into the store. "See that? I know he heard me," said Puggley. "Man, everybody knows that Tony is gay. Why does he have to get so mad when somebody says something?" asked Puggley. "That's his little brother, Puggley," I said. "And you know how Antoine is about Tony; he promised his mom that he would look out for him." "Well, if he really wanted to look out for him, he would make him not come out in those women clothes, and," but before he could finish his sentence, Antoine came out and popped the trunk. I looked at Puggley and asked, "Aren't you going home first?" "Yeah. But first, I'm going to the hotel and hit a home run with my girl. My folks don't know. They think that I won't be coming home for another three days. I'm going to spend the first three days with my girl," said Puggley, looking at her, winking. He then laughed at me, saying, "I told you not to break up with Roxanne; when a man comes back home, he wants something warm to lay with." Then, after punching me in the arm, he simply said, "See ya!" and jumped into the car with Pam. She blew her horn, waved, and sped off toward downtown. "What did he say? A man needs to come home to something warm," asked Antoine, rhetorically. "Well, he's right about that; I mean, when he says something, he means something, because that grizzly bear that he calls his girl is big enough to keep the whole team warm, and ugly enough to win first prize at the monster ball." "Come on, man," I said, laughing with him, and then adding, "At least he has someone." "What are you trying to say, Sam? That I don't have anyone?" Antoine snapped back. "I'm not trying to say anything," I replied. "Actually, I was talking about me and my breakup with Roxanne." "What's wrong with you, man? You've been on edge ever since we left the base," I added. But Antoine just dropped his head, mumbled something, and then said, "Forget it, man. Let's go down to the strip club and have a drink." "That sounds like a winner to me," I said, then adding, "Wait. Let me go into the store and get some change." "For what?" asked Antoine. "I need some one dollar bills in case I want to make it rain," I replied. Antoine laughed and said, "Hurry up, will you?" I jumped out and ran inside the store.

I entered the store and was standing in front of the candy racks when two guys came in. One of them bumped into me with so much force that I felt the sidearm that he had inside his belt. My first thought was to say, "Watch where you are going!" but then I remembered how the Major had stressed how important it was to stay out of trouble. My next thought was that this might be some sort of test, so I just ignored him, grabbed a peanut chew bar, and headed toward the cashier. But, as soon as I took my first step forward, the second gunman appeared in front of me! He didn't bump me, but his body was angled so that it was clear that he had a 44 magnum pistol tucked in his belt. Although I had received a boat load of training, I didn't need it to recognize that these guys were not cops. As much as I was tempted to say something, I decided to mind my own business; however, when you know that someone is up to no good, you have a tendency to keep an eye on them, and that's what I did as I walked toward the cashier. "Hey, Sam," Antoine yelled out as he walked in, causing me to flinch. "Grab me a Hershey bar; I'll save you a spot in line." At that point, Antoine was standing in front of the cashier, and beside the second gunman; behind the second gunman was yet another gunman – the third gunman! I didn't know what was going to happen next, but I stopped and looked at the two gunmen standing at the cashier station, and then at Antoine, trying to give him some sort of warning; but he looked back at me and said, "Can you hurry up?" I then turned toward the candy stand and the second guy pulled out his 44 magnum and said, "You stand right here and give up the money." I glanced at Antoine to see how to handle this, but the second and third gunmen had their guns drawn on him, and the third gunman shouted, "Everybody empty your pockets! And you, open that drawer!" to the cashier. "Hurry up!" he added, and then slapped her with his gun. In one quick motion, Antoine caught hold of his wrist, and put the third gunman in front of him. As he was doing that, the second gunman tried to put himself in position to help his friend; but Antoine, still holding onto the third gunman, spun around and kicked the second gunman in the mouth so hard that three of his front teeth went flying! By, now, the first gunman, who had pulled his gun on me, was about to make his move. I waited for one second as he took his aim off of me and tried to point his gun at Antoine. I then stepped to the left, and, with a front hand blade chop to his throat and a knee to his groin, I grabbed his gun hand, and turned it up his back until I could hear his arm snap like a dry twig. He dropped his gun, and I quickly took control of the gun and turned toward Antoine; but he had subdued both gunmen, and was looking at me with a smile, "You got him, boot!" I was shaking like a leaf on a tree, but Antoine was as cool as a cucumber in a fridge.

Within seconds, Baltimore city police were on the scene. I laid the pistol down on the floor and backed away with my hands over my head. I looked at Antoine, but he did not look up; instead, he just mumbled, "this is f--ked up." Immediately, the store manager explained to the officers what had just happened, and labeled us as heroes. I thought it was pretty cool, because, by the time the officers had finished questioning us, the TV news cameras were everywhere. When Antoine and I walked outside, a reporter approached me, but Antoine yanked me by the arm, saying, "Come on! We got to get out of here!" As we were getting into the car, a news lady with a mike ran up to us and said, "I heard that you two Marines took down three heavily armed gunmen, and saved the day! You want to tell us about it?" Antoine replied in a voice that I

28

had never heard before; it was real country. "Ma'am, we're not heroes. We were just passing through on our way home to Alabama." His head was down as he spoke. "We've got to go, ma'am," he said as he put the car in reverse and backed out of the parking space. He then tipped his baseball cap to the news lady, who, in turn, threw her business card inside and said, "Call me"; but Antoine did not look up as he sped off to I 295 South.

I sat there watching him talk to himself, repeatedly saying "we f--ked up. This is not good." Finally, I said, "What the hell are you talking about, and where are we going?" "We screwed up, Sam. We should have never got involved!" shouted Antoine. "Hey man, how the hell did we know that those assholes were going to do something like that?" "I knew," said Antoine, adding, "I saw them when they got out of their car toting guns. I first came into the store to warn you, but then, when I saw one heading back toward you, I knew we could take them. And the adrenaline rush that I got was not going to allow me to do anything but what I did. You can't tell the Major that, or he'll bust me and kick me off the team." "Man, there were women and children in there! Certainly the Major will understand that; plus, they were threatening our lives," I said. But, just as I said that, both of our phones rang at the same time. "Shit! Shit! Shit! That's the Major!" said Antoine, banging on the steering wheel. I looked at my phone and, as Antoine had predicted, it was the Major. The text read, "Meet me at the BWI Hilton in forty five minutes." "How the hell can he know about it that that fast?" I asked. "The last thing he said was to keep a low profile," he answered. "I know that, Antoine. But how could he know about something like that that quick?" "Our names are on every Intel and law enforcement agency around the world; so, if one of our names pops up on airways, it sends an alert to the command center, and they contact the unit commander. Well, so much for leave," he said. "What do you mean?" I asked. "We'll see what the Major says,

Antoine replied, and within seconds Puggley called and said, "Man, I just got a text from the Major saying that we have to meet him at some hotel at BWI. What the hell is that all about?" "Tell him to just meet us there!" said Antoine, as he kept looking back through the rear view mirror, and then slowed down to allow a few cars to pass us. I noticed that one of the cars was the same car that had been parked beside us at the store. When the driver drove past, he did not look over, but just sped by.

Antoine turned off at the first exit. We saw car break lights immediately ahead, but we were in the far left exit lane. Antoine took the exit around to get back on I 295 South heading toward BWI airport. We got to the hotel just as Puggley was pulling up. He kissed his girlfriend on the cheek, climbed out, and came over to our car. "Man, is this some kind of training test?" he asked. "Because, if it is, this is f--ked up; I haven't spent any time with my girl." Antoine got out of the car and looked around as if trying to determine if someone was watching us. Then he looked at his cell phone, read a text message, and said "Come on, the Major is already here!" "But how can he be here?" I thought, "Because it only took about twenty minutes to get here." As we walked into the hotel, Puggley continued to ask what this was all about, but Antoine never said a word all the way to the elevator. We stepped off the elevator at the top floor. By the expression on Antoine's face, I knew that whatever this was about was not going to be good. We knocked on the door and Stoney answered, looking at Antoine. Shaking his head, Antoine quietly said, "I know."

"Know what?" asked Puggley.

"I know, or, should I say that I knew it was a bad idea for me to let you and that fat ass senator talk me into this family and friend commando team," said Major Travis as he walked out of the bathroom. "Major, I can explain," said Antoine. "Explain what?" asked the Major angrily. "You're out!" he said. "What?" Antoine gasped. "You heard me! Out! Let me spell it for you: Capital O U T, out! What the hell were you thinking? You've been compromised. Look," he said, pointing at the TV. And there we were on every local news station in Baltimore. "I've got to sit you down for at least a year," said the Major. "And my bosses are telling me to demote you and send you back to the sleeper unit." "Major, I worked hard to get into this position," said Antoine. "If y'all were knuckle heads, that would be something I could explain; but you've been on too many missions to make this type of dumb ass mistake," replied the Major, adding, "So it's settled; you're off the team for six months, and pray that no one has recognized you." "Were you followed?" the Major then asked. "No, I don't think so," said Antoine, nervously. "You don't think so?" said the Major. "Either you were or you weren't!" snapped the Major. "No, sir. We weren't followed. One of the news team people tried to follow, but I lost them on I-295," replied Antoine. "Well, find a place to bunk on the floor, because nobody leaves this room until tomorrow morning," said the Major. "But sir, my girl is down there waiting for me," said Puggley. "Then you need to call her and tell her to go home, because you won't be coming back out." "I don't have my phone on me. I left it in the car," said Puggley, telling the Major a lie in hopes of being able to go downstairs to at least briefly see Pam. But the Major quickly responded, saying, "Well, if you truly left your cell phone in the car, you will have to sit down permanently, because that means that you also have been compromised, not to mention that your cell phone is your life line; and that means that your girl is probably going through your numbers right now, so we will probably have to kill her, too." "Oh, wait! I have it, sir," replied Puggley, holding up his cell phone. "Good, Lieutenant. I didn't think that you would make a mistake like that. You men make yourselves at home," said the Major.

31

Then, turning to Antoine and walking toward the balcony, he said, "And you, send your girl away, or would you like for me to send Stoney down to tell her that you won't be coming back down." "No, sir," said Puggley. "I'll call her," he mumbled, adding, "Man, you guys can f--k up a wet dream," as he walked into the bathroom to call Pam.

We sat about two hours, watching TV and waiting for Antoine and the Major to finish talking. The Major was really laying into Antoine. We couldn't hear specifically what he was saying, but, from the tone of it, the Major was really pissed. Five minutes later, Antoine stormed back in from the balcony and headed right out the door. I wanted to asked him if everything was alright, but he had that "don't ask me shit" look on his face; so, I just waited for the Major, because, if he was that pissed with Antoine, who had been in the unit for over six years, I kind of had an idea what he was going to do to me.

The Major walked in from the balcony, looked at me, and then shook his head with disgust, saying, "Stoney, call it in. Antoine has been sat down, taking effect immediately." Stoney hesitated for a moment and looked at the Major with disbelief. "Is something wrong with your hearing, Marine? Barked the Major. "No sir!" replied Stoney, as he made the call to the unit command center. From that point until six months, or whenever the Major decided to let him back in, Antoine was pretty much on his own. Now, I had only heard the term 'sit down' one time before, but everything was happening too fast. I still had not seen or heard from my brother Sal. Now this. The Major looked at me and said, "You'll be briefed on everything in the morning. Until then, nobody leaves this room; we'll be in the adjoining room."

As the Major and Stoney left, I could hear Stoney say, "With all due respect, Major, don't you think that sitting him down was a little hard?" "Are you questioning my judgment?" asked the Major. "No, sir. I'd never do that. I just know that Antoine is the best member of the team," replied Stoney. "You think I don't know that!" the Major snapped back. "But this cousin and friend thing seems to be messing up his judgment; it could easily have cost him his life, and the life of Sam as well," added the Major. "I'm going to take another look at these videos. I didn't see enough of Sam's face that anyone could get a facial recognition on him; but Antoine's mug is all over, and, if that's not enough, his martial arts moves were shown so that anybody who sees it will know that he is not the average Marine. And, right now, it's being viewed all around the world." "I see what you mean," replied Stoney, adding, "Well, let's get on the horn to the damage control unit."

"What the hell's going on?" belted out Puggley, scaring the hell out of me. He then paused and said, "Were you eavesdropping on the Major's conversation? I hope so, because somebody needs to tell me what the hell is going on, and why I have to be grounded because you two wanted to play hero." "That's not what happened," I replied. "Well that's what I'm seeing on the TV. Why didn't you guys call me back so I could have had some fun, too?" taunted Puggley, then adding, "Whoa!" as he saw the news video of Antoine subduing the gunmen. He then said, "Man, you guys sure are glory hogs!" He kept rewinding the TV, saying, "Man, this is some Hollywood-made-for-TV shit!" I looked up at Puggley eating his sandwich and pointing at the TV. Then I got in the one bed, exhausted, and fell to sleep almost instantly as the Major and Stoney viewed the tapes (as were practically all of the terrorist organizations around the world).

The tapes were bright red flags to antigovernment agents and agencies. The two items that make a hero are bravery and ability;

the two play an important, interconnected role. It's one thing to be brave enough, but one must also have the ability to perform. And, for the level of ability that Antoine showed, it was clear to experts that it required special training – more than that of a regular Marine.

The morning came early. It was about 4:00 am when we pulled out. I thought that I was going to be dismissed right along with Antoine; but, instead, the Major said, "Good job." I didn't know how to handle that, so I just said, "Thanks," and looked over at Puggley, who looked back and hunched his shoulders. The Major sat in the front passenger seat, Stoney drove, and Puggley and I sat in the back. About a mile into the trip, the Major called my name, turned around, and asked, "Do you know why I said 'good job' to you, but sent Antoine home?" "No, sir. Not exactly," I replied. "Well," he said, "when you subdued your man, you took him out gracefully, and never looked up, so we could replace you with anyone at the news conference; but Antoine's face was all over the TV. I got there too late. They won't show it again today, but let's hope and pray that nobody noticed him last night. Your cousin is a true hero – not because of last night, but because of the countless bad guys that he has put away. And now, because of that one stupid mistake, I have to pull him out for a while. When we get back to Camp Lejeune, I'm going to need a full report on everything that happened from the time you walked into that store, right up until everything went down. You understand?" "Yeah. I understand, sir," I replied. "Good," he said, leaning back in the seat and pulling his cap down over his eyes.

But, as we headed back to Camp Lejeune, Tony and his new friends were heading to Baltimore. We were just on the other side of Richmond, VA when my phone vibrated; it was Antoine. "Hey, Sam. Sorry about that bullshit. I didn't mean to f--k your leave up. I know how much you wanted to spend some time at home," he said. "Yeah. Well, you're right about that," I replied. Then he said, "Wait a minute. Someone here wants to talk to you." "Who?" I asked. Then he put her on. "Hi, Sam," she said in the sweetest voice. "April!" I said. "Yes," she responded. "I came up here to spend some time with you." I didn't know what to say, so my first thought jumped out. "Can you come back down here?" I asked. "Down where?" she replied. Then Antoine got back on the phone and said, "Don't worry, Sam. I'll show her a good time." "Tony and his crew just got into town," he added. "How long are they going to be up there?" I asked. "I don't know," replied Antoine. "Tony's supposed to be taking over some new nightclub downtown and also opening up a karate school right here in Baltimore. I'm thinking about going to work for Tony at the nightclub since I have some time off. But don't tell the Major. I mean, I know that, eventually, he's going to find out!" Then he added, sincerely, "By the way, what I said about 'showing April a good time,' I meant that; and that's without putting a knife in your back, so you don't have to worry about that." "I know, man. I just wish I had come out of that store when you first told me," I replied. "Well, what's done is done, and we'll let damage control clean it up," he said, then adding, "You just concentrate on the training program and get a completion so that we can welcome you guys into the team." "Hey Antoine, you said 'you guys'; now, does that mean that you want Puggley to complete it as well?" I asked. "Of course," he said. "Puggley is a good Marine, but he just doesn't know what to say out of that big mouth of his; and if you don't watch out for him, he's going to trip right over those big lips of his, and say the wrong thing to the wrong person. But I got to go," said Antoine, hanging up the phone.

Months went by, and I still hadn't heard from my brother Sal. The Major briefed us when we first got back – about getting involved in civilian affairs while on leave, and how to conduct ourselves; and that's when I realized that everything that we had done within the store had been 100% wrong. But, with all of his briefings, he had never told us where Sal was, or what Sal was doing. Every now and then, I would get a call from Antoine telling me how much fun he was having back in Baltimore.

Tony had the number one gay club in Baltimore – maybe even number one on the East Coast; and all of his staff were experts in the martial arts. They were his handpicked, personally trained, gay men and women. The club was set up to make money. It hosted both gay and straight customers. Furthermore, he indicated that Tony was about to become a millionaire from the club alone, not to mention all the other side businesses he owned – such as a karate school, and two or three beauty salons (with partners), as well as a quiet marriage recruiting firm for gay and lesbians seeking partners from different countries. Antoine said that the marriage recruiting firm was the most lucrative business outside of the club; it matched single gay people together faster than they could say 'I do.' Tony's gay marriage services were so hot that he had two paid appearances on The Ellen Show, and was supposed to do Oprah in the fall. His greatest popularity and exposure came from matching a U.S. Senator from New York with a young Prince from the Middle East; it made news around the world, and featured Tony as being 'at the top of his game.' Then, they featured him in TIME MAGAZINE – in big bold print over and under a picture of Tony on the front cover, in which it showed him jumping into the air with two fists each clenching a fat wad of $100 bills, and with a big smile from ear to ear. Even his dad was featured in a photo with him on an inside cover story. But, no matter how much money Tony made, or how popular he became, Puggley still felt the same way about him – often expressing it as, "He's still a fag. He's just a rich one now." As I was reading the article on Tony, Puggley walked past, and I asked, "Man, why don't you quit hating on Tony?" "What?" Puggley asked "Are you jealous of him or something?" I added. "Who, me? Jealous of him? For what? He's got all those girls around him, and can't even get it up! Who wants to be jealous of someone like that?" asked Puggley. "Yeah. What about all that money he's making?" I asked. "Yeah, he is getting paid," Puggley agreed, looking at Tony's picture on the front page of Time Magazine. "You would think that he was having the time of his life, but there is a dark side of Tony that he can't seem to pull himself away from, or it won't detach itself from him," Puggley added.

CHAPTER 3

Dealing with Adversity

"Come on, Paul! Let's take a trip to Baltimore. I have received some disturbing news, and it demands my immediate attention," said Freddie, as he stood on the balcony of his mansion on the coast of Africa.

Freddie had seven mansions that he spent time in, but the one in southern Maryland – though far from being the most extravagant – had the most beautiful, breathtaking structure. It was a giant brick plantation designed with two swimming pools – one indoors, and one almost Olympic-sized in the backyard. The seven-bedroom mansion rested on forty acres of land, and included a manmade lake and a horse farm. It was truly a fortress due to its protection by video cams, human motion detectors, and four security dogs that ran loose about the property.

It was a late Saturday night when they landed in Baltimore, a bit too late for Freddie, who decided to go straight to his southern Maryland mansion.

But, in Baltimore at "the club," the party was just getting started. Antoine called me around 12:45 that night. We had just gotten in from what was going to be our last I.T. class. After the third ring, I answered the phone, "Hello." "Hey, Sam. What's up with you?" asked Antoine, sounding as if he might have had one drink too many. "Man, its 12:45 and we just got back in," I said, yawning. "Yeah. I know," he said, adding, "You guys are probably just coming back from night Interrogation Training." "Yeah. How did you know that?" I asked. "I wrote the book on it," said Antoine, adding, "You see, boot, there's a difference between night

Interrogation and day Interrogation; hell, there's a difference in that at noon, too, but you'll learn that tomorrow. Who's teaching the class?" "You know that I can't tell you that," Sam responded. "Just checking, boot." Somebody shouted in the background. "Who was that?" I asked. "Here, I'll let you talk to him." "What's up, Marine?" "Sal?" I asked. "You got it!" he responded. "Sal!" I yelled out. "Man, where have you been? I was beginning to get worried! Where the hell have you been?" I asked again. "It's like you told Antoine; you know I can't tell you that, but the Major can and will in a couple of weeks when you boots graduate," said Sal, then adding, "Oh shit! He slapped the hell out of him!" "Who, Sal?" I asked again. "Who slapped the hell out of who?" "Tony. Come on, Sal," I heard Antoine say in the background. "Let's get the hell out of here." "What's going on?" I asked. "It's nothing. Tony and his crew are putting some guys out of the club," he responded. "But he beat him up pretty good, so Antoine and I are heading out the back door. I'll call you when I get in the car," said Sal as he hung up.

I didn't find out until later what had happened, but the word I got was that a young lady and her gay brother had tried to pick a fight with Tony because Tony had once dated her brother's lover, who had been all over Tony in the club a week earlier. The story was that the young lady approached Tony, saying "I should kick your narrow ass for messing with my brother's friend." Reportedly, Tony looked at her as if she were crazy and asked, sarcastically, "Did you take your bipolar medication today?" April then walked up to stand beside Tony, at which point the young lady looked at April, saying "Bitch, what do you want?" But April uttered not a word in response, but simply looked at Tony with a question on her face, as if to say, 'what's up?' or 'what's wrong with her?' And, when Tony and April glanced at each other, the young lady took a swing at Tony, saying, "Is this your bitch?" April then caught her fist, twisted her arm to completely dislocate her shoulder, and replied, "No, bitch! I'm his bodyguard!" as she threw her onto the floor while her brother watched. After the young lady was helped to her feet, she started shouting, "You must not know who I am! My daddy is Little Mickey, and you are going to pay for this shit!" "Well, you go tell Little Mickey how you got that hickey, and let him bring his fat closet ass down here. I promise you that he will get it worst," said Tony, waving goodbye to the young lady as she was escorted out the door.

True to her word, she went straight to her father – a big time drug king pin with ties to many of the most powerful gangsters on the East Coast. He resolved to avenge her, sending four of his goons to confront Tony. The smallest one of the four was six feet four, and two hundred eighty pounds. When they got to the door of the club, the doorman said, "Check your tools, just in case," (talking about their pistols). "Man, we probably won't even need any heat. I mean, it's a gay club," said one of the men. Then, the biggest man of the four grabbed his dick, saying, "Yeah. How hard can it be?" All four laughed heartily, and bullied their way through the door, the biggest man saying to the doorman, "I brought you a present from Little Mickey," and, WHAM! He hit the doorman in the mouth, knocking him out cold; he then flinched at a guy with whom he had been talking; the big man chuckled as the wimpy dude fainted, saying, "It's like I said. How hard can it be?" He laughed and grabbed his dick again, but all hell was about to break loose because the doorman was also Tony's live-in lover.

The four men got about ten feet inside the club when they were quickly surrounded by Tony and his crew; the music stopped, and Tony got on the mike, saying, "We are sorry for the brief intrusion, but I would like for all my club guests to please retire to the upstairs ballroom while we handle an uninvited intrusion." So, all the customers were escorted upstairs, and Little Mickey's goons were faced by six scrawny, small gay guys and one woman, April. Then Tony shouted out, "Ramone! Oh my God, Ramone!" "Who did this?" asked Tony, running over to help Ramone up wiping the blood off his mouth. "Little Mickey had a present for you. I guess he gave it to the wrong guy or gal," said the man, laughing. Tony helped Ramone over to the bar. "I'll take the second part of that message," said Tony as he approached the big man. "Well, here it is," the big man started to say; but, before he could finish, Tony delivered three strong, perfectly placed kicks that totally incapacitated the big man. And Tony's guys made quick work of the rest of Little Mickey's crew; in fact, they beat them so bad that they had to drag them out into the back alley. And that's when they discovered Antoine and Sal – both shot. Antoine had been shot twice, once in the leg, and once in the shoulder; but Sal's one shot had been fatal, passing through his heart. Antoine called out for Sal, but Sal was dead. "Call the ambulance!" screamed Tony.

Within seconds, the police were there because someone had called them when they heard gun shots in the alley. Police cars pulled in from both directions. But Tony, in a rage, ran over to the big man, ripped his gun out of his holster, and pointed it at the big man's head – shouting, "You killed my cousin!" But the police drew their guns, pointed them at Tony, and screamed, "Drop your weapon!" Tony hesitated, and the officers raised and pointed their guns at Tony, saying, "This is your last warning! Put it down!" "Tony!" screamed Antoine, pleading with his brother. "They killed Sally!" Tony shouted again, and, just when one officer was about to shoot, a ranking officer came running to the forefront, ordering, "Hold your fire! Lower your weapons!" as he walked up to Tony. "Give me the gun, Tony. We'll take care of these assholes," said the officer in a clearly gay voice, as he took the gun and put his arm around Tony. With Ramone looking on, Tony knelt down beside Antoine, took his hand, and began to cry. "Why did they shoot you? Why did they kill Sal?" Tony asked. Then, a plain clothes detective said, "I need everyone to stay here for questioning." Antoine passed out while they were loading him into the ambulance.

Before the first news flash, Major Travis had received the horrible information about his Marines, and, because of the high security level of Sam and Puggley (still in their final month of training), the Major purposely neglected to tell Sam about the slaying of his brother – leaving that job to his mother. But, because the Major and Sal had been good friends, not being able to tell his brother for security reasons grieved him deeply. Sam received "the call" from his mother at about five am – telling him that his brother had been shot to death by gang members. "Mom, that can't be true! I just talked to him a few hours ago. I told him that I was coming up there next month. Momma, say it's not true!" Two seconds later, Puggley burst onto the scene and stopped, watching Sam weep for his brother. Shortly thereafter, Sam received a call from the Major, ordering him to stay on base until he returned; but Sam was numb with disbelief that his brother was dead, and killed by a gang of street punks. Sam was so full of rage and remorse that none of the Major's conversation made any sense. Sam stumbled, sat down, and dropped his phone to the floor. By now, Puggley's eyes began to tear up as he rushed over to his best friend's aid. He embraced Sam and shouted in a killing tone, "We gonna get them motherf—kers!" Then Puggley picked up Sam's phone. He heard the Major screaming violently. After some hesitation, Puggley answered the phone, "Hello." "This is Major Travis, your commanding officer," he said, then adding, "look out your window." "I'm in Sam's room," said Puggley, sarcastically. "Well, I don't give a damn whose room you are in! The whole building is surrounded with eight sentries with orders to shoot anyone trying leave that building. This is for your own safety and the safety of every Marine in that building. Everyone is grounded there until we can find out what the hell happened. There is no liberty for anyone." "Put Sam on the phone!" he added. "Sam's not in a talking mood right now," replied Puggley. "Well, put me on speaker so both of you can hear this, because I'm not going to repeat it. An investigation has begun. Those gang members will be dealt with by the laws of that state," said the Major. "Whose law, Major? Yours?" asked Puggley. "I'm going to pretend that I didn't hear that," replied the Major, adding, "You guys sit tight. I'll be there in less than an hour." "Sit tight?" said Sam. "Somebody just killed my brother and shot my cousin, and you're telling me to sit tight!" Sam yelled out, adding, "He wasn't just my brother, but was supposed to be yours, too! Remember? This unit is a team of brothers! You said that, sir! It was your words!" "And they are still my words," said the Major, cutting him off. "But we are still Marines, Lieutenant! And don't forget that! I know that you are hurting right now; we all are, son. But we have to let the laws of the land prevail. I've already contacted the 2nd Marine Division chaplain to arrange for humanitarian leave for you and Puggley, but with special provisions." "What the hell does that mean?" asked Puggley. "NCIS has to do their investigation so just sit tight. I'll explain it when I get there, Sam and Puggley. I'm very sorry that this happened. Sal was a good man, and an excellent Marine. I'll be there shortly," said the Major before hanging up.

There was a surrealistic stillness in the air that night as Sam and Puggley sat in Sam's room, quietly talking among themselves. "I think the Major knows what happened," said Sam. "Why do you think that?" asked Puggley. "Why else would he put us on lock down?" replied Sam, adding, "He might even have had something to do with it." Sam started to get emotional. "Whoa! Whoa!" said Puggley. "You're just upset, Sam, and you are letting your emotions take control of you." Then, Puggley added, "I think the

Major can be an asshole, too, sometimes, but there's no way I can even begin to imagine the Major doing something like that!"

Silence fell over the room again, this time for about thirty minutes. Then Sam, finally agreeing with Puggley, said, "You're right, man. The Major would never do nothing like that." "I know I'm right, Sam," said Puggley, adding, "How do you think we got into this unit? You think Antoine got us in? His mad ass couldn't even get us in the club that time; it was Sal who got us in. He and the Major were very close. He and the Major's sister were about to be married," said Puggley. "What?!!! How do you know that?" asked Sam. "Sal told me." "Why didn't he tell me?" asked Sam. "I don't know. But you know that Sal always told me stuff that he'd never tell you. Besides, because of our unit creed of law, he wasn't supposed to tell anyone. Sam, you know the rules." Puggley then added, "They were supposed to have gotten married next month when we graduated. He was waiting for you to come and be his best man." Puggley fought back tears, and Sam sniffled and took a deep breath. Then, Puggley stood up and said, "Hey, man. I've got a fifth of jack and six beers; I don't know about you, but I need a drink." Puggley headed to his room as Sam sat there quietly in the partially lighted room – pondering everything that had happened over the previous five hours. His thoughts were interrupted when Puggley walked back into the room and turned on the light. "Kill that light!" said Sam, trying to focus his eyes. With only the light from the television and the dimly lit hallway, the two best friends then sat down on the side of the bed and poured a drink. As both of them raised their glasses to toast Sal, the Major walked in. Both Sam and Puggley stood up, but the Major quickly said, "At ease," and sat down beside them. We could see the disappointment and sorrow in his eyes as he reached over to get a cup off Sam's table, and began to pour himself a drink. The three of them sat on the side of Sam's bed and raised their cups in a toast to Sal. After a moment of silence, Sam asked, "What the hell happened, Major? Why is my brother dead?" The Major poured another drink and said, "So far, what we know is that your cousin Tony had some sort of dispute with some local gangster named Little Mickey, who supposedly sent his goons over to rough up the place; but, apparently the tables got turned, and the club's security beat Little Mickey's guys to a pulp. And, after dragging them into the alley, they discovered Antoine, shot twice, and Sal, dead from one shot to his heart at point blank range." The Major looked into Sam's eyes to make sure that he was capable of handling the graphic truth. Sam's eyes teared up once again, and he poured another drink. Puggley poured himself another drink, too, and sat the bottle down on the dresser. The major then latched hold of the fifth, saying, "I'd better take this with me, but you guys can finish off these beers," as he grabbed two of the beers. Finally, he added, "We'll set up the guidelines for your leave in the morning. I know it's hard, but try to get some rest, and I'll see you in the morning."

Puggley stood up and looked at Sam as he answered his phone. "It's Pam," he said. "She's also a little upset about this shit." Sam just nodded his head. "Are you going to be alright?" Puggley asked. "Yeah, Puggley. I'll be fine," replied Sam. "Close that door for me, please." "Sure, man," said Puggley as he walked out of the room. Almost before the door had closed, Sam broke down and began to cry intensely. Puggley stood outside the door briefly before the tears began to run down his face, too; then he quietly walked to his room.

The morning came with no sleep for any of them – not even the Major, who had sat up most of the night drinking. It took two days to get the official leave papers in order. By the time Sam got there, Tony had arranged everything. The "home going" services were fit for a president, but none of the team members were allowed to attend – not even Sam; but they were allowed to view the body at the parlor, but only with a unit team member.

On the day of the funeral, over forty limos showed up with some of Hollywood's biggest gay stars, who showed up at Tony's request. Not just actors, but also big name athletes, senators, congressmen, two governors, and some of the most influential people in the free world. It was truly a great send off, but there were still many unanswered questions, such as, "Why was the killing blamed on a street gang? Why, two days after the funeral, was Little Mickey killed in a drug raid?" People in the city called it 'poetic justice,' but the word on the street was that Tony had gone in with the police raid dressed as a cop and shot Little Mickey ten times in the chest and face; but that story never reached the news media. In addition, it was claimed that all the cops who raided the house were gay and lesbian police officers.

CHAPTER 4

Business as Unusual

At the six-month point after Sal's murder, no one talked much about it, and the police believed that – with Little Mickey dead, it was an open and shut case. But the deep wound of his brother's death left Sam with a huge amount of bitterness and anger, mainly directed toward those who break the law.

This was their third raid on the drug cartels in Central America. It was approximately 20:50 military time. The I. I. E. team had surrounded what they believed to be the home of one of the top men within the cartel and a major distribution depot; so, to be able to capture him, the drugs and the money – well, this was going to be a good catch! As they quietly locked themselves in position and waited for the 'go' sign from the Major, five young ladies came walking out, got into a limo, and drove off. "You want me to stop them?" Puggley asked from his roadside position. "No! Stay low and let them through. They are just the guppies that the big fish in the house are feeding on, and the big fish are the ones we want. So, stand by and wait for my signal," replied the Major. "The Christmas tree is lit, Major. I say again, the Christmas tree is lit," repeated J.J., which meant that all the explosives were set and ready to detonate. "Let's make it happen, fellows," said the Major, leading six of his Marines plus fifteen agents from D.E.A. and Homeland Security. They stormed the house with very little resistance. There was one low-in-rank cartel front man, plus six guards; they killed four of them, but they soon realized that the big fish they were looking for had escaped with the women. After locating a ton of weed, about a hundred pounds of cocaine, and over two million dollars in cash, they started ripping the house apart to see what else they could find on other members of the cartel. The Major was super pissed because, obviously, someone had tipped them off! "I got Intel three hours ago telling me that Mr. Big himself was here; there must be a rat on one of your teams," said the Major, talking to the team leaders from D.E.A. and Homeland Security. "You wait a damn minute, Travis," said the D.E.A. agent, adding, "I wanted this S.O.B. just as bad as you, but I'm not going to accuse members of my own team of some bullshit like that. Nor will I take that from some dumb ass Marine like you!" "What did you say?" the Major asked, as he turned toward the D.E.A. agent. Puggley moved in, standing behind the Major for support, and J.J. moved in to the left. The D.E.A. team then started to move in to support their leader when the leader from the Homeland Security team stepped in between the two groups, saying, "In spite of popular opinions and high testosterone, I'm in charge of this raid, and I won't let us be blindsided by that freak escape."

"Major, you might want to take a look at this," said Sam, as he viewed the surveillance video. "It shows all of us on camera from two miles out. It even shows J.J. setting the explosives in place. The faces of our entire I.I.E team were masked with paint, but complete facial recognition parameters were exposed – meaning that the names and addresses of every D.E.A. agent and Homeland Security officer involved in the raid were thereby exposed!" "Who's the dumb ass now?" the Major asked, as he and other team members went outside to look for security cams. Finding no cams, the D.E.A. team leader asked, "If there are no cams, how the hell did they take these recordings?" "I think I know," said the Major. "And if I'm right, unless we correct this right now, all of our agents across the globe will be exposed." He attempted to reach his commanding officer at the Pentagon. "How the hell could he get that technology?" the Homeland Security team leader asked. "I don't know," responded the Major, "but he has it." "Has what?" asked the D.E.A. team leader. "It's high technology that the U.S. Government just developed. It's a microscopic spy and defense security system," said the Homeland security leader. Finally, the Major said, "The Pentagon is confirming it now through satellite imagery surveillance." "Copy that," said the Major, talking to someone on the other end of the phone; then, he said, "Sparkie, go outside and turn off the power. Puggley, go with him. J.J., if it takes more than five minutes, blow it up. Everybody, turn off your cell phones!" "Why?" one guy asked. "They are going to send an E.M.P. through satellite command," said Major Travis. "Major!" J.J. shouted. "We've got a problem!" "What is it, J.J.?" "I'm reading hot spots all over this freaking place." "Of what type?" asked Major Travis. "H.E., Major! High explosives everywhere!" said J.J. "Grab them two assholes. Everybody get the hell out of here! NOW!!!" shouted Major Travis, as he headed to the door. "Let's move! We have about two minutes before the satellite sends that pulse. They knew we'd figure it out and called it in. They're going to use the pulse as a detonator for the H.E. Move it, move it!!!" the Major shouted.

As everyone ran to the outer court yard, one of the two surviving cartel guys broke free, pushed the D.E.A. team leader to the ground, and ran back toward the inner court yard. The Major turned around, looked at the D.E.A. team leader lying on the ground, and shouted, "Let him go! Come on!" as he ran, looking back. "Go ahead," the D.E.A. team leader said, adding, "My ankle is broken." The Major, without missing a step, turned around, ran back, and said, "Come on!" offering his hand. When the agent stood to his feet, Major Travis bent down, scooped him up onto his shoulders, and started running. He managed to just make it to the outer court when the E.M.P. went off. Puggley and two D.E.A. agents hurried to help the two men to a safer distance as the whole complex blew!

The air was littered with construction debris, cocaine, and money – most of it burnt beyond recognition, but with a few un-burnt ones as well. Sam and Puggley pocketed a few of them for themselves. "Alright, pack it up, boys," said the Major, adding, "Bring that asshole with you, Puggley. And if he tries to run, shoot him."

It was a long walk back to the portable command center, and a long trip by chopper to the base camp in North Carolina by way of Langley and the Pentagon. "We'll take him from here," said the Homeland Security team leader. "I don't think so," said the Major, adding, "This man is a murdering drug dealer, so I think that my team and the D.E.A. should have the first crack at this guy. And, if I were you, I'd be more concerned as to how they got their hands on top secret materials and info that haven't even been used by us yet." The D.E.A. team leader quickly agreed with Major Travis, and then quietly thanked him for coming back and probably saving his life. The major just nodded his head and said, "It's all good. Get that ankle looked at. My buddy here and I are going to have a nice little conversation." He leaned close to the prisoner's left ear, and said, "Come on, buddy," as he walked him to the interrogation room and slammed the door.

"Now, I know that you are a low down piece of shit drug dealer, and I also know that you are a cowardly murderer; that comes from a long lineage of garbage just like you. But, what I don't know is, where would a two bit 'yes man' like you get that technology; and that's what you're going to tell me, or I'm going to cut off your eyelids, and then I'm going to extract your teeth, one by one. Do you understand me?" the Major asked. But the man did not speak, so Sam spoke up, saying, "Maybe he can't speak English," as he helped secure the man to the chair. Sam then asked him the same question in Spanish, but, even with the Spanish, he still did not speak. "Tape his head to the back of the chair so it will be still," ordered the major. Sam asked the prisoner for the last time if he understood; speaking in Spanish, but no reply came forth. The Major then walked over to him and said, "Last chance, asshole." The man just smiled, and then finally spoke, saying, "You can't do anything to me because you have violated my rights by taking me from my country and threatening me with bodily harm." "Threat? You think that was a threat?" asked the Major, as he picked up a pair of tweezers and a razor blade. "You think that you can scare me?" the man asked. "I don't know," the Major replied, as he took hold of the man's eyelid with the tweezers, pulled the top lid out, and cut the lid completely off. The man screamed in agonizing pain. "You still think I'm bluffing?" asked the Major. And, before he could answer, the major lashed onto the other eyelid, pulled it out, and once again swiftly cut it off. "Looks like you won't be getting any shut eye tonight," said the Major. "Now, before I start pulling teeth, I have decided that I want to start with a manicure; but, just like your teeth, those finger nails cannot be saved; I'll have to rip them off, one by one," said the Major as he latched the needle nosed pliers onto the prisoner's left thumbnail. As he was about to yank the nail off, the prisoner screamed out, "Okay, okay!" "Okay what?" asked the Major, yanking off the thumbnail. "Please, please!" the prisoner cried out as blood ran down his face and hand. "Please what, motherf--ker?" asked the Major, about to pull another nail. "Boss, I think he's ready to talk," said Puggley, looking at the Major. "Yes, yes, yes!!!" said the prisoner.

"Sam, you and Puggley get our gear ready. We're taking this garbage to Camp Lejeune with us." "That's not the deal," said the D.E.A. agent as he walked into the room. "I'll give you thirty more minutes with him, but I can't let you take him," he said. "Well, thirty minutes will be enough," said the Major, then asking, "How's the ankle?" "Just a hair line fracture. I'll be fine," he responded. "Good!" said the Major, and closed the door.

Later, in the briefing room, the Major explained why he had asked the two men to leave the room.

It was about 0500 when the Major walked into the briefing room. "Wake him up," said the Major, pointing at Puggley. Sam elbowed Puggley lightly. "Listen up," said the Major. "I'm only going to explain this once. My boss doesn't want me to explain this to you at all, but, because you've already been exposed to it on a mission, the Pentagon has given me permission to explain it to you in detail," said the Major, as he began to explain further.

"The Microscopic Spy and Defense Security System, commonly known as The Eye in the Dark," was developed during Desert Storm, but there were no trees or tall posts in the desert; however, they were able to deploy it on roof tops, and on the top of mountains in Afghanistan. The mobile units were good for monitoring the activities of our troops, and also warning them of hidden dangers that they could not see. But, somehow, this scum has gotten his hands on it, and everyone whose face was exposed – well, let's just say that, by now, whoever was running the show over there, has every bit of information that there is to know about them – right down to where their momma lives. And, because we don't have enough Intel on this guy," said the Major, "he has the advantage over us. Until we find out how much Intel has been leaked, they've asked me to secure all liberty until that can be determined." "What?" Sam and Puggley asked at the same time." "Come on, Major," said Puggley. "We've been locked down since Sal's murder," he said, looking at Sam; but Sam just dropped his head, and leaned forward in his chair. Puggley quickly apologized to Sam for bringing up the bad memories, but the Major interrupted by saying, "Look, that's what they want me to do, but I didn't say I would. I do have another plan, and that is that you guys can go home for the weekend, plus four, but you're going to have to wear disguises so that no one can recognize who you are, especially if you are going to be visiting your gay cousin's night club, because we still don't have all the reports on everything that happened that night. Sam sat up straight and asked. "What are you saying, Major? They still don't know who killed my brother?" "All I'm saying is that we don't have all the facts yet, so I'm going to need your word that you can follow that one simple order. And, keep in mind that we will be packing up and heading back out on another mission on Monday; so, that means that I will be expecting you guys back no later than 2200 Friday evening, 10:00pm." "Do I make myself clear?" asked the Major. "Yes, sir!" they all replied.

We slept most of the day. It was about 6:00pm when Sam heard Puggley banging on the door. "Come on! Get up, Sam! The week will be over before we even leave!" "Alright! I'm getting up!" Sam yelled back. The two of them had not been home for months – not since Sal's death.

The ride up from North Carolina was quiet. One of the Marines from Sam's old unit wanted to hop a ride with them to D.C., so Sam agreed; but, on the way there, he began to ask a lot of questions about Sam's unit. Of course, Sam just led him to another conversation. When they were about to drop him off, he tapped Sam on the shoulder and asked, "Hey, man. Does your cousin still own that club in Baltimore?" "Yeah," said Sam. But he wondered how he knew about it, and then thought, "Hell! Tony's all over the news. How could anybody not know about it?" The Marine got out on Pennsylvania Avenue and said "Alright, fellows. I'll see ya, but I wouldn't want to be ya!" "Whatever, man," replied Puggley, as the Marine closed the door. "Why does he always say that dumb crap?" asked Puggley, adding, "Ain't that the same guy who had that beef with Sal that time?" "You mean when we first came out of boot camp?" "Yeah," replied Sam. "What was that all about anyway?" asked Puggley. "I don't remember. That was almost four years ago," replied Sam. The two then stopped at a McDonalds to grab a bite, put on the faked beards, and change clothes.

It was about 10:30 pm when they pulled in front of Tony's club in Baltimore.

"Man, if my girl sees me dressed like this, she's going to think that I've flipped the script. Hell, if anybody sees me dressed like this they are going to think I've flipped," said Puggley. "So, let's make this quick so I can hurry and get to the motel and meet with my girl." Both men were dressed in what they considered gay costumes. Sam wore black bell bottom pants, a lime green shirt, and a plaid sports jacket. Puggley wore purple pants, a pink shirt, and a black tie.

Their disguises were so good that they were able to walk right past Tony's friend Ramone, and sit at a table beside Tony, without him even noticing them. He was telling a story about Oprah Winfrey, and how he had conned her out of a free subscription of O Magazine. "Child, I sent Oprah a letter telling her that I couldn't afford to pay for the magazine, and she gave me a year's worth free. Then she found out who I was and asked me for a thousand-dollar donation for her favorite charities." "So what did you do?" his friend asked. "I gave! What else would I do? Hey, it's Oprah!" said Tony, adding, "I thought I had done something significant, but she added a hundred thousand to it, so I said 'Oh well; so much for my Nobel peace prize!" Tony laughed, and then said to the gay man that he was sitting with, "Look at that fine thing that just walked in here! He's going to make me gussy on myself." Puggley mumbled, "That's just nasty," adding in a whisper," I know that your cousin is gay and all that, but why does he have to be so gross?" Sam smiled through his fake beard and said, "That's just Tony." "Yeah. I know," said Puggley as he ordered another drink.

They sat for about an hour before Tony noticed them, but it came by way of Antoine, who walked in and right over to them with a big smile on his face. He walked right past Tony and went straight to the table where they were sitting, leaned over to Sam, shook his hand, and whispered, "It's not Halloween yet, but those are some pretty nice outfits." He then shook hands with Puggley. "How the hell did you recognize us?" asked Puggley. "I'm trained to recognize; besides, your hook up is not that good," said Antoine, looking at Puggley's purple shirt.

Tony stood up, excused himself from his guest, walked over to the table where they were sitting, and, with a big smile, said," I want to scream, I'm so excited to see you guys; but with the look that 'Toine just gave me," he said, speaking of Antoine, "and from the way you guys are dressed, I have to assume that you must not want anyone to know who you are, so I'll just play along." Tony then hugged both men brotherly, and sat down with them. "What's up with you guys?" asked Tony. "I haven't seen you all in months," he added, and then asked Antoine, "Did you make the deposits today?" "No," Antoine responded, adding, "I'll do a night drop." Then, turning to Puggley, he said, "Come on, meat head. I know that you don't want to be in here anyway." Puggley agreed and slid his chair back from the table, and then leaned over to Tony, whispering, "That was some gutsy shit you did to Little Mickey. We all appreciated that." "Well, I didn't do anything," said Tony as he winked at Puggley, "but he had it coming." "Yeah, cool," replied Puggley. Then, leaning over to Sam, Puggley shook his hand and said, "I'm out." "Where you going?" asked Sam, as if he needed to ask. "I am going to ride to the bank with Antoine, and then I'll have him drop me over at my girl's house." "Like that?" asked Sam, looking at his clothes and smiling. "Oh, no! Maybe we can stop somewhere so I can change," he said, and was about to walk away when the guy that Tony had been talking to approached him and asked, "How would you like to be a part of my photo shoot?" Puggley looked at him and said "A photo shoot?", "Yes!" The man replied, "You are perfect," adding, "I'm doing a story on gay men who are afraid to come out of the closet. You would be perfect because you don't even look gay." Sam chuckled as he watched his best friend try to get away. "I' m not ga—" Puggley started to say, and then changed it to, "good, that's what I mean; I'm not good enough for something like that, but my buddy sitting right here is," pointing to Sam as he walked away; but the guy followed him all the way to the door. Tony and Sam laughed as Tony said," Puggley is still the same." "Yeah," said Sam. "He'll never change," and then added, "He's right, you know; we all do appreciate what you did." "Yeah. Well, he had it coming, but I'm not so sure that he acted alone or had someone else in on it, said Tony. "What do you mean?" asked Sam, getting excited "Wasn't he the one who sent them goons to your club?" "Well, yes," said Tony, hesitantly, "but a friend of mine who knew Little Mickey said that someone had approached Little Mickey, but he turned them down." "Turned him down for what?" asked Sam, getting loud and angry. "Sshhhh!" said Tony. "Alright, alright!" said Sam, trying to calm down. Sam then asked, "What are you saying? That Sal was a target?" "I don't know," replied Tony, emotionally, adding, "All I know is that one of my police sources said that they are investigating some young kids from the east side who were bragging about doing a drive by on two guys, and it was blamed on Little Mickey. They call themselves 'New York T.H.C.'" Tony added, "But they don't have any association with the gang called T.H.C. here." "How do you know any of this to be true?" asked Sam. "Look around," said Tony, and then added, "You see the guy sitting at the end of the bar talking to April? He's from a gang called the Eastside Lords. You see the three sitting in booth to the right? They are in a gang called the Westside Boys, and the little fellow talking to the doorman – well, he's with the real T.H.C.

gang. He's been trying to recruit Will for the last two months, but he doesn't know that Will is gay. All the rest of them that I just mentioned – well, they belong to my gang, the Gaylords. Sam took his eyes off of April and looked at Will, admiring his six feet eight height, and his roughly three hundred twenty pounds of solid muscle, asking, "He's gay?" "And can fight his ass off," replied Tony, further adding, "among other things, of course," as he smiled. Sam said, "Of course," and added, "but how does he know?" "Because I had Will ask him, and he's so desperate to recruit him that he shared everything," said Tony. "I know it's 'he said' - 'she said,' but the word is that the T.H.C. gangs are out to get them for pretending that they were T.H.C.; and when they find them, they are going to kill them," said Tony, adding, "and that's fine with me." "But why would anyone want to kill Sal and Antoine?" "I don't know, Sam," said Tony, with tears in his eyes. "I just don't know." "Well what about your police friends? What are they saying?" asked Sam. "They are just as baffled as you and I are. One of the kids got shot last night during a shoot out with an off duty police officer. My source says that they haven't been able to question him because the feds have him under strict security," added Tony. "Why would the feds be involved?" asked Sam. "I don't know," replied Tony, "but I believe that it has something to do with Sal being in the military"; he then added, "My friend said that some Marine corps major was pushing his weight around, and now no local cops can even get close to him." "Tony, will you do me a favor?" asked Sam. "What's that?" replied Tony. "Did he ever say where those guys hang out at?" asked Sam. "Why, Sam? You're not going to do anything stupid, are you?" asked Tony, "Because you need to let the law do their job. My friends on the force will catch them."

"So how is April doing?" asked Sam, changing the subject, then adding, "She's still as pretty as ever. I'm sure that she is seeing someone else by now." "No, indeed!" said Tony, with a smile. "You left that girl's nose so wide open that you and Roxanne could spend the night up in it together." "Oh yeah?" asked Sam, pondering Roxanne; "Now that's a thought. How is Roxanne doing "Don't ask me," replied Tony, "because she's in her own world with some dope addict from out of south Baltimore." "When you say 'addict,' Tony, do you mean like a pot head or something?" asked Sam. "No!" responded Tony, "He shoots dope and coke, and smokes crack." "Why do people f--k themselves up like that?" asked Sam.

"There are many reasons why people go through what they do," responded Tony, adding, "If you were to listen to some of their stories, you might understand." "I doubt that," mumbled Sam. Then, Tony took a deep breath and said, "Anyway, take your girl, April. She really likes you, but I don't believe that she has had sex with anyone because her daddy started raping her when she was six, and didn't stop until she was twelve when she killed him in his sleep." "Wow!" said Sam, "you mean she really killed her father?" "No, silly soap," said Tony, "but she said that she wanted to kill him. She said the lady next door called the cops on him, and child custody took her out of the house, and locked his bitch ass up. Then, there's my friend Ramone; every time his mom left for work, his step daddy raped him and beat him really bad. Then, when he told his mother, that whore also beat him, and told him that it was his fault and that his step daddy was just drunk and that he only did it because Ramone was cute and looked like her; but she allowed that shit because she was strung out on dope. You see the waiter on the far end of the bar? His filthy ass mother has been having sex with him since he was eight years old," then adding, "and, believe it or not, that bitch still comes in here and demands that he come straight home after work! Now how nasty is that? And he's so psychologically screwed up that his mother is the only person that he has ever had sex with." Tony then continued, "He had a boyfriend, but she not only ran him away, but anyone else who dared come into his space."

"Well what about you Tony? I don't recall anyone abusing you," said Sam. "Hell no!" replied Tony, twisting and turning in his seat, then adding, "I just choose to be gay." "Well, on that note", said Sam, "I've got to go. Tell April that I'll be back later." "I was just kidding about her killing her daddy," laughed Tony. "I know," said Sam, smiling, "but I really do have to go." "Hey, Sam!" yelled Ramone, trying to be heard over the loud music. Sam waved and continued out the door.

Tony beckoned to Ramone, and they walked into Tony's office. As Tony put the key in the lock, Ramone reached out and grabbed a generous handful of Tony's ass. Tony shivered and turned to kiss his lover, but quickly remembered why he had summoned him, and then, kissed him on his cheek, and said, "We'll finish this later, but, right now, I need you to follow Sam; and call me if he goes on the eastside – especially if he finds those little murdering pieces of shit before we do; and take April just in case your need some support!"

Ramone slapped Tony on the butt cheek, looked at April and nodded. She immediately broke off her conversation with a customer and followed Ramone. The two got into April's new Corvette and took off behind Sam. Although they kept a good distance behind Sam, his training had taught him very well such that he spotted them after he made his second turn. By not knowing who was tailing him, he figured that the only logical thing to do was to find out who it was and why they were following him. He could have lost them, but he wanted to know who it was, and didn't want to lead them to his parents' house. So, after leading them all over Baltimore City, he slowed down to a crawl, and pulled into Druid Hill Park, where a night run for The Cure for Cancer program happened to be in progress. Sam drove through the park slowly as people walked by, but, once they had passed, he sped until he got to the Howard Rawlings Britannica Garden Building. He quickly parked and got out, reached into the trunk, grabbed an old sweat shirt, put it on, and began to walk in the opposite direction, mingling with the crowd. He walked right past Ramone and April, who were looking out the window for him. Sam quickly pulled out his phone and called Tony. The phone rang ten times, and went to Tony's voicemail. "Tony," said Sam in a calm voice, "you need to call me right now." As luck would have it, Tony walked into his office just as Sam was finishing his message, and picked up his phone before Sam hung up. "Sam, is everything alright?" asked Tony, in a panic. "I don't know," replied Sam. "Should I ask April and Ramone?" "No, Sam. you don't have to ask them," replied Tony, "I just don't want to see you get yourself into any trouble, or worse; but, if you promise to go home, I'll call them off," said Tony. "Alright, 'cuz," said Sam. "That's where I'm going."

Tony quickly called Ramone, and laughed, saying, "Come on back. You bitches have been busted." By then, Sam was approaching his car, and was about to open the door when April pulled past, slowed down, and tapped the horn lightly. Sam leaned over slightly and said, "Nice car," as she smiled, waved, and pulled off.

Sam had a few things on his mind. For one, how did Ramone know that that was him behind his disguise? And, could that major be Major Travis? These were questions that had to be answered, he thought, as he drove to his mother's house.

April followed Sam to his parents' house, and then drove off as he pulled into the driveway. "How do you think he knew we were following him?" asked April. "Dude, he saw us," said Ramone, adding, "I told you to let me drive." "Yeah, right!" said April, driving down North Avenue. When they reached Pennsylvania Avenue, the light turned red. Just as she stopped, a group of young guys standing on the corner shouted at April, so she quickly put up the windows. "Can you put my window down?" asked Ramone. "Why?" asked April. "Look at them with their pants hanging down off their asses." "Yeah!" said Ramone, "like they are ready." They laughed as three guys approached her car. One ran around to her side and began to try to make conversation; the other two walked to the passenger side and started pointing their fingers at Ramone, saying, "You're a blister! Look yo, that's a faggy." Ramone looked at them and casually said, "You're the ones with your pants hanging down below your butt cheeks, like you are waiting for me or somebody to put something up in you." April and the two other guys laughed at Ramone's remark, but one young man, who instantly became enraged, cursed at Ramone and threw his almost-full beer can, hitting Ramone in the chest, and spilling beer all over him, April, and her brand new car. When the light turned green, April sped through the light, and stopped on the other side of the intersection, parking in front of a library. "That's why I didn't want to put the windows down," said April, as she got out of the car.

The three guys, seeing that she had stopped, and joined by one more guy, raced over to her car. April was leaning over her seat, drying up the beer, when one of the guys walked right up behind her, grabbed his dick, and said, "Girl, I'm 'bout to put something up in you." The other three walked up to Ramone, one of them saying, "Yeah. What's up now?" April looked at Ramone and said, "You're going to explain this to Tony." "Alright!" replied Ramone, getting out of the car. Backing up, April straight back kicked the guy behind her in the chest, and then two- pieced him with a left hook to the side of his head and a right cross to his jaw; he was out in an instant. It happened so fast that the other three stood there,

mesmerized and amazed. Then one of them said, "Bitch!" and
pulled his pants up and started to walk around to April. But
Ramone grabbed his shirt tail and said, "Hey, big fellow! I thought
you wanted to play with me." Then, the other two stepped toward
Ramone and, like a whirl wind, Ramone spun around and kicked
both of them into a waiting April. "But, I've got something special
for you," said Ramone, looking at the last man standing. The young
man reached down, pulled his pants up, and Ramone slapped him
twice in the face, at which point the fellow put up his fists, as if to
box, so Ramone put his fists up, too; but, with lightning speed,
Ramone kicked him under his chin, and, as he stumbled backward,
Ramone quickly hit him in the gut, pulled his pants down to his
ankles, and pushed him onto the ground. Ramone then landed
three hard kicks in his ass, and went over to the other two who
were trying to get up; he snatched down both of their pants to their
ankles, and delivered ferocious kicks into their guts. "Come on,
Ramone! Get in the car!" yelled April. The one that she had two-
pieced was still out cold in the middle of the street. When Ramone
got into the car, she quickly pulled off, and they started laughing.
"Really, Ramone! You just had to pull their pants down?" said
April, laughing. "Well, they should have put on belts and pulled
their pants up," said Ramone, smiling, "plus, I thought maybe one
of them might have had something to see." "You're sick," said
April, smiling as she drove back to the club.

The morning came early with Sam's phone ringing off the hook
with his ring tone screaming, and annoyingly repeating, "Get up,
motherf--ker, get up mother--ker," and increasingly loud with each
passing ring; finally, on the tenth ring, Sam fought his way from
under the covers, almost falling out of bed to reach his phone
before the caller could hear him say, "Hello, hello." "Man, did you
see this bullshit?" "What?" asked Sam, adding, "Who is this?"
"That's a dumb ass question," replied Puggley. Sam yawned and

asked, "What the hell are you talking about, Puggley?" and what time is it anyway?" "It's 0630," replied Puggley.

"6:30!" Sam shouted, then asking, "Why the hell are you up so early?" "Why are you not?" asked Puggley, in a slurred voice. "Why I'm not? Wait a minute! Are you drunk?" asked Sam. "I better be drunk – all that damn money I spent in Tony's club on booze; we're supposed to be on R and R. You know, Rest and Relax." "And what the hell were you doing at Tony's? I thought that you didn't like gay people." "I don't," said Puggley, "but, you remember Pam's brother Melvin?" "Yeah. What about him?" asked Sam. "He's gay." "Melvin?" asked Sam. "Are you sure?" "He kissed Tony on the lips," said Puggley. "No shit!" replied Sam, then adding, "Didn't you two spend the weekend together down at National Harbor a few years back?" "What?" snapped Puggley. "You know – the time Pam got mad at you and left you and Melvin down there for the weekend. As I recall, she turned in the key to yours and her room, and you were forced to stay in the room with Melvin for the whole weekend," said Sam. "That was before he was gay," said Puggley. But Sam interrupted, asking "Why are you calling me 'man?'" "Something funky went down with Sal that the Major is not telling us about," said Puggley. "Like what?" asked Sam. "I'm not sure, but Melvin said that Sal might have been on some sort of mission." "Well, we knew that," Sam said," but how did Melvin know?" "He asked one of his people that overheard his boss say that it was some sort of joint, multitaskforce with all types of feds. But no one knows who the taskforce was after. So, what makes you think Sal was involved?" asked Sam. "Why was the Major one of the feds in the meeting?" asked Puggley. "How do you know that?" asked Sam. "Get your tired ass dressed and come over to Pam's house and I'll show you. I've got his bad ass on T-bo," replied Puggley. "I'm going to get dressed, but you sober up. I'll be there shortly." "Sober up?" responded Puggley. "I thought that you said you were on R-R." "Well," Sam began as Puggley cut him off by saying "Jack-up, man. I'm drinking coffee as we speak."

Chapter 5

Making Sense out of Nonsense

Sam hurried, got dressed, and sneaked out quietly. As he raced over to where Puggley was staying, he couldn't help but think of his dead brother. Tears of anger and grief filled his eyes as he pulled up in the driveway. He noticed a car with two people sitting inside, parked across – at the other end of – the parking lot. At first glance, they looked normal; but, after a double take and watching them watching him, Sam was thrown into a very suspicious mode. So, he decided to walk over to where they were parked. When he was about thirty feet away, the car pulled off with two suited persons in the front seats. As they drove off toward the morning sun, Sam could not get a read on the license plates because of the brightness of the sun rays, but he quickly took out his cell phone and snapped a picture of the plates, turned, walked to Puggley's door.

"Do you want to tell me what the hell you are talking about?" asked Sam, as Puggley opened the door. "Hi, Sam," said Pam, as he walked in, adding, "Would you like something to eat or some coffee?" "Yes, coffee's fine," said Sam as he sat down at the kitchen table. "Look at this," said Puggley, rewinding the T.V.; he then said, "Who is that?" – pointing at the person on the T.V. "That's my baseball cap – the one that the Major took from that kid on our first mission. Remember?" As Sam looked closely, he began to remember the words that the Major had said when he took the hat from the kid; he had said, "Give me that cap; you're not a baseball player, you're a drug dealer," and had added, "I'll keep the cap, you keep the cuff," as he put the kid in the van. Sam's forehead began to sweat as he said to Puggley, "Play it back again," and, finally, "You're right. That is Major Travis. What the hell is going

65

on?" "That's what I want to know," said Puggley. "I think it's time we had a talk with the Major," said Sam as the three of them sat in the kitchen drinking coffee. Then, a knock came at the door, and silence fell over the room. Puggley and Sam looked at each other as Pam got up to answer the door. Both men sat quietly, waiting to see who was at the door. When Pam returned, April was with her. "Hey guys," said April as she walked in. Puggley hurriedly changed the T.V. channel. "Hey, April," said Sam, "You're up early!" "Well, you have to go to bed in order to get up, and I haven't been there yet," she replied, and then said, "I thought you were coming back to the club last night." "Well, I was, but I was being tailed, and it took me almost all night to shake them," said Sam. Then, Sam looked at April and smiled. She smiled back and said, "I only came over to tell you that Tony is having a party at his house tonight, and he wants you guys to come. Now, I'm going home to go to bed." Sam slid back from the table, got up, and said, "I'll walk you to your car." As the two of them walked out, Puggley stood up, turned his head left to right, and said, "Look at him. He's like a lamb heading to the slaughter." "Well, he deserves someone nice," said Pam. "Nice? You call that nice?" asked Puggley, then whispering, "A nice body, and I do mean a nice body." "Oh, thank you, baby," said Pam, thinking that he was talking about her; so she went over and gave Puggley a hug. The two then kissed, standing at the kitchen window, and then Puggley released his kiss long enough to get a last peep at April's beautiful, perfect body.

As the two made their way to the bedroom, April was about to get into her car when Sam noticed that same car, that had been at the far end of the parking lot earlier that morning. The car was now parked about four blocks up the street. He quickly stepped closer to April and said, "Would you do me a favor?" "Sure," replied April, "What is it?" "Would you kiss me?" asked Sam. April looked at him with wonder, and then Sam started to explain about the car parked down the street, and said that he wanted them to be distracted into believing that he had not noticed them; but before he could finish telling her his rationale, she practically jumped into his arms, and kissed him with fiery passion. Within seconds, Sam forgot why he had asked for the kiss; instead, he went for a deep, mesmerizing deep throat passion that lasted for a very hot five-minute stretch. When they released, they were engulfed in the passion of their bodies pressed against each other. Sam cleared his throat, and stuttered briefly as he said, "You going home, huh?" "Yeah," said April, "To go to bed?" asked Sam, "Would you like to come with me?" Sam gave her a sweet kiss on the lips and said, "Sure!" By then, both could feel Sam's hard penis pressing up against her soft body. And, while the two were wrapped together, they were suddenly interrupted with a loud yell. "Hey! You two cut that out or get a room!" shouted Puggley, as he banged on the kitchen window.

Sam looked down the street to if the car was still parked there, and, sure enough, it was still there. Sam was now beginning to come back down to earth; he snapped back to reality and looked up the street. "Do you see that car parked up there, the black one?" he asked. "Yeah, I see" she replied; "Well, I'm gonna leave and drive in the other direction." "But, when you drive past, take a picture of them clowns, and send it to me, and I'll meet you downtown," said Sam. He then pulled April in close to him again, and asked, "Do you think you can do that without them noticing what you are doing?" "Are you kidding? That's easy. I thought that you were going to ask me to stop and kick their asses; and I would gladly do that if you wanted me to," said April, with a smile on her face. Sam leaned over, kissed her again, and said, "You are so gorgeous." Then he asked again, "Are you sure that you can do this? Don't make me wait too long!", April said. Getting into her car, "Don't worry, I'll be there before you, and I will get the photos for you, too!" Then, just as she had promised, she gently slowed down and pretended that she was looking into her mirror, while secretly taking their pictures; but, they made it easy for her because they were captivated by her stunning beauty. The two men intently scoped her out while she clicked away – taking four photos without them noticing. Furthermore, she waved at them as she drove past them.

Sam acted as if he had never noticed them parked in the distance, and walked back to the house. As soon as he got inside, Sam shouted, "Puggley, come down here!" "I'm already down here," said Puggley, walking from the kitchen, and adding, "Boy, I seen you busting spit with your girl April. She's a fine young thing. And when she threw that thing on you, your whole head could have fallen off." "Puggley," said Sam, in a serious voice; but Puggley, still feeling good from the night before, kept on talking over Sam: "You know, she has one of those Beyonce things going on; I mean, she's fine up top in the face, and built all the way down to her bottom – everything in the right place. And that's why J.Z. bops his head up and down – he can't help it; one moment he's looking at that beautiful face, and the next moment he's look down at her fine body." "Okay, Puggley. I get it," said Sam, grabbing Puggley by the shoulders, and finally getting his attention. "There's a car with several dudes out there, about four blocks up. You can't see them from the window, but they are out there, and they were out there when I first pulled up. April took a few pictures as she drove by, and just sent them to me. I'm going to take a little trip." "Alright, give me a couple of moments to grab a few things; I'm going with you," said Puggley, putting his coffee down. "No," said Sam. "No?" questioned Puggley in a highly irritated tone. "What the hell do you mean by 'no?'" "I said 'no' because I need for you to draw them off my tail." "Alright," agreed Puggley; "What do you have in mind?" "Go get your kit; mine is in the car," said Sam.

Puggley raced upstairs and returned with his makeup artist kit. Just as Sam was about to grab a handful of hair from Puggley's kit, his phone rang. It was April, saying, "I'll meet you here." "There's been a change of plans. Can you meet me at the Patapsco Light Rail station?" asked Sam. "Sure," replied April. "How long will you be?" "As soon as I can," replied Sam; "And, April, don't park on the parking lot. I'll meet you on the street underneath the bridge, and then we'll call Tony and tell him that you and I will be hanging out for the weekend." "Cool," replied April as she hung up. "That's pretty smart," said Puggley. "Yeah. I figure that, if you put on my clothes and drive off in my car, they'll follow you, thinking it's me," said Sam. "Yeah. That will work; but I'm talking about you taking April with you. That's quick thinking," said Puggley. "Yeah. I figured she could help me with the driving," replied Sam. "Driving my ass. You mean that you plan to do some driving – deep up into her thing," said Puggley, as he took Sam's hand, saying, "That was a slick move, homeboy." Sam quickly snatched his hand back and said, "Give it a rest, will you?" "Why you bluffing, Sam? I saw the way the two of you kissed out there – like you guys have been doing that forever," said Puggley, laughing. But Sam hurriedly said, "That was a diversion." "Bullshit!" said Puggley. "Are you trying to tell me that you didn't feel anything when you kissed that fine ass girl?" Sam smiled and said, "Well, I guess I felt something." "You felt something! Is that all?" asked Puggley. Sam looked at Puggley, smiled, and burst out laughing, then saying, "Man I can't lie; my dick was harder than all get-out." "I know," said Puggley; "Shit. My dick got hard just watching you guys." "Hey, hey!" said Sam, cutting off Puggley. They both laughed and then got serious with changing clothes and putting on their disguises. Sam made himself up to look like Puggley. "Man, that does not look like me. You've got way too much beard," said Puggley. "Hell, they are parked four blocks away," countered Sam.

"They have a fix on my clothes, so that's where their focus will be. So, go outside, get in the car, and go!" "Where do you want me to go?" asked Puggley. "Take them north. I'll call you when I meet up with April" "Alright, cool," said Puggley as he stepped outside, jumped into Sam's car, and pulled out. Sam, standing at the window, verified that the car followed his car with Puggley in it. Then, as soon as they turned the corner, Sam ran out, got into Puggley's car, and sped off in the opposite direction.

While Puggley played cat and mouse with his chasers, Sam called April, and asked her to meet him at the Patapsco Flea Market, which was closer, and which would have hundreds of people walking about – just in case they had to blend in order to lose a follower.

Sam arrived just in time. As April got out of her car to watch the entrance for Sam, she was approached by the same young guys who had been at North and Pennsylvania Avenue. They walked straight over to her. The tallest one walked up to her and said, "Hey trick, you wanna try that shit now while I'm still sober?" But, before she could answer, Sam called her from his cell phone as he drove past where her car was parked; then, he parked about ten spaces down. When her phone rang eight times, without April answering. Sam started thinking, "Come on, girl! Get off the phone!" He called again, but, still no answer. Sam, in Puggley's car, then darted into a nearby parking spot, as he tried again to reach April on the phone; but, still no answer. Sam then jumped out of the car and started walking down to where April was standing. Once he got about five spaces beyond several tall vans, he could see April in what he thought was a fight for her life. Sam charged toward them like a pit bull after an alley cat; but, before he could even get close, April had made minced meat out of all three. Sam stood there in amazement, looking at April, and then said, "Are you okay?" She looked at Sam and raced into his arms,

"Should we act like we don't see whatever it is that you do, huh?!" asked Sam. "Just kiss me, silly," said April as she kissed him. Sam could not fully enjoy the kiss because of the three young men lying on the ground – knocked out cold. "Hey, miss! When you guys get done, can I take a picture of you?" asked a middle aged man who was standing there with his cell phone. "Let's go," said Sam, pulling away, but not letting go of her hand; he then lead her to her car. "Ma'am, I'm a photographer for the Baltimore Sun. I saw the whole thing; they started it, and you kicked the shit out of them." Everybody that was standing nearby agreed by applauding loudly. "Yeah! I got that shit on cell cam," shouted one person. But April and Sam just got into the car. Then, she abruptly opened the door and stepped out. By then, the three guys had begun to wake up. "Hey!" Sam yelled to April, "What the hell are you doing?" "I just want to say something to them," responded April. "I think that they probably got the message," said Sam, watching them trying to reach a stable stance. "Just so you jerks know, you can't go around picking on defenseless women and gay men, because we're fighting back," said April. Then, someone in the crowd whispered, "Oh. he's gay!" "What?" said Sam, looking around the crowd. "Can we go now?" asked Sam, then noticing a security patrol van heading toward them.

"April," said Sam, nodding his head in the direction of the approaching security van. "Can we go now?!" "Yes." "But just one more thing," said April to the three, "If I ever hear about you bothering good people again, I'm going to come back and have this big nigger throw you down on the ground and fuck the shit out of all three of you in front of all of your friends." "I really don't like that word too much," said Sam, taking hold of April's hand as she was getting back into the car. "What word? 'Fuck?'" asked April, smiling. "No," he replied. "The N word." April put the car in drive, looked at Sam, and said, "Everyone says it here." "That's because they don't know any better, and I doubt if half of them even know what it means," said Sam with dismay. April looked at him and said, "I can tell by your face that you really don't like that word, do you?" "No. I really don't," said Sam. "And I think it's a shame that people go around calling each other ignorant bastards all day, and think that it's something to be glorified! By the way, what the hell was that all about back there?" asked Sam, changing the subject. "Which way?" asked April as she reached the highway. "South," said Sam, and

asked again, "What was that all about back there?" "Them nig.." said April, cutting the N word short. Then, she smiled, looked at Sam, and said, "Them bastards threw beer in my car last night while we were at the stop light at Penn and North, and hit Ramone in the chest; so, we kicked their asses." April then continued, "And, because I was by myself, they thought I would be easy pickings." "So, in other words, you are a small potato, but are hard to peel," said Sam, smiling. April smiled back and said, "I was thinking maybe a cherry, because that's small, too. Right?" asked April. "Yeah," replied Sam. "But who would want to peel a cherry? I think one might want to savor the inner and outer parts in order to get the full favor of the whole cherry." "Ooo, I like that!" replied April, smiling at Sam as they headed south toward North Carolina.

Chapter 6

Searching for Clues

April drove until they reached Richmond Virginia. And then, for the third time, Sam asked her to pull over and let him drive. When she finally did, she could hardly keep her eyes open.

Sam was about to pull off when his phone rang. It was Antoine, so Sam hurriedly answered. "Hey, Sam! How are you guys?" asked Antoine, without a greeting. "I'm alright. How about you?" asked Sam. But, before answering, Antoine said, "Oh, my bad cuz. I was just wondering why you guys would leave when Tony is having a party tonight." "Oh shit!" said Sam, adding, "I've got to hang up; there's a cop behind me!" Sam quickly cut off Antoine and laid his phone on the console as the police cruiser drove past, but Antoine continued to call as the officer began to put some distance between them. Sam was about to call Antoine back when Puggley's ring tone came through again. "Hey, Puggley! How are you? Is everything alright?" asked Sam. "Yeah, man. I'm good," Puggley responded, and then said, "Code 10." "What are you talking about?" said Sam, giving him the proper response to the Code 10. "I say again, Code 10, Go," said Sam, giving the proper answer. "Nobody," said Puggley. [All of those Code 10s and answers meant, "Don't trust anyone with the information that I'm about to speak": and Sam understood them very well.] Then, Puggley said, "Man, things are crazy up here right now. You know those assholes who were following me? I lost them in Atlantic City, or they got my info and stopped tailing me. But Tony just called me and said that the Feds just raided his house." "What were they looking for?" asked Sam. "They didn't say," replied Puggley. "Well, what did it say on the warrant?" asked Sam. "It was a blank, open warrant of search and detain, with no names," said Puggley, "so, you know what that means." "Yeah, I do," said Sam. "Whoever they were looking for must be pretty high up on the food chain, but who would Tony know like that?" asked Sam, rhetorically. "I don't know, dog, but there's some weird shit going on," said Puggley. "Yeah! You can say that again, because a Virginia State Trooper just popped up behind me from out of nowhere, and, shit, he's pulling me over. I've got to hang up," said Sam. "Wait, Sam," said Puggley, adding, "Don't forget protocol; take a picture and send it, and watch your back, because, like I say, there's a lot of weird shit going on." "Alright," said Sam, placing his phone in a position in which he could record the face of the officer approaching from the driver's side. But, just as he took his hand off the phone, two more police cars approached – one from the front, and another from the rear.

A total of six police cars parked. Cops jumped out with guns drawn, and more pulled up behind them. In addition, two helicopters hovered overhead. "Sorry, baby," said Sam, "but you've got to wake up." April sat up to see what was going on, and asked, "What did you do, run a red light or something?" "No! I didn't do anything!" "Alright, driver of the vehicle, place both hands out of the window, and passenger on the other side, you do the same," blurted a megaphone. "Oh shit, Sam. I've got some weed in my purse," said April as she turned toward Sam. "Okay, that's not good," said Sam, then adding, "Just be cool and do what they ask." While both Sam and April hung their hands out of their respective windows, the officers slowly approached their car with their guns pointing directly at their heads. "Don't move!" the officers warned. They moved in on April's side, quickly cuffed her, and escorted her out of the car. Then, a fat state trooper slowly walked up to Sam and asked, "Do you have any weapons on your person, or in your vehicle?" "No," replied Sam, as he then looked at April, standing outside the car, and whispered, "Do we?" She shook her head 'no.'

"No sir, officer! We don't have any weapons! Can you tell me what this is all about?" asked Sam. "Take her back to your car," said an officer, talking to two female officers. "Hey!" said Sam, starting to get out of the car. "I am going to have to shoot you if you try to get out of that car!" said the officer, looking Sam in the eye; he then said, "Let me see your license, registration, and insurance card." Sam took a deep breath and reached into the glove compartment. "Slowly, slowly," said the officer, adding, "We're not going to hurt your little girl friend, or whatever she is." He and his buddies chuckled, and Sam began to explain to the officer that the car he was driving was not his, but belonged to April. However, the officer cracked another joke by asking Sam, "Is your name, April?" Once again, the officers had a nice little laugh, but Sam was not in a laughing mood.

Sam began to count how many cops there were, and started scanning the highway and the off road routes to identify possible escape routes. In his mind, he had already grabbed the closest cop and reversed his gun, and then used him as a human shield while he gunned down the rest. Sweat dripped down the side of his face, and. just as he was about to put his plan into effect, his phone rang a special override ring that only the Major had. By now, Sam was looking around, and side to side; then, after the fourth ring, he hit the answer button, but kept silent. The Major broke the ice by saying, "I know what you thinking right now. Your heart's racing, your adrenalin's off the charts, and you've already plotted your escape route and how you'll mow down ten country cops! You know that it's just a walk in the park for you because you know that you can drop all ten of them in twelve seconds. But, you're not going to do that, are you, Sam?" asked the Major. "What the hell is going on Major?" "I'll explain it to you when you get to Lejeune. They won't bother you again." "Get the fuck off of me," said April, getting back into the car with Sam. The two female police officers looked at the lead cop and shook their heads, as if to say 'no.' "Are you sure?" said the fat lead cop as he handed Sam his stuff back. One of the female cops then said, "We ought to know." "Yeah. You ought to. Come on, let's get the hell out of here," said the lead cop, then mumbling, "A waste of tax payers' money."

"What did they want with you? Did they hurt you?" asked Sam frantically. "No. A little humiliated, maybe," said April. "What did they want with you?" Sam asked again. April looked at him, took a deep breath, and said, "They wanted to see my kitty cat." "Your kitty cat?" said Sam. "Yes! My kitty cat, couchie, twat, Cody cat – you know, my pussy," said April, getting upset. "Why would they want to see that?" Sam asked, then adding, "I mean, I'd like to see it, too! I mean, well, you know what I mean." Trying to cover for his tripping over his words, Sam added, "I mean, they actually looked up inside? For what? Drugs?" "No, silly. They were looking to see if I was actually a female." And, with breaks in his voice, Sam asked, "And what result?" With a playful smile, April asked, "Are you asking me to do the same thing for you?" as she looked deviously at Sam. "No," replied Sam, as he glanced at April out of the corner of his eye. Again, as Sam was about to pull off, she looked at him, smiled, and said, "I guess we'll find out tonight." "Find out what?" asked Sam. "Hmm," said April, leaning the seat back and pretending to fall back asleep. "Now that you two love birds have finished discussing female anatomy, you can take me off the speaker." "Oh yeah! 'Sorry, Major!" said Sam, taking the phone off the speaker and putting it to his ear. "I don't have to say Code 10, do I?" asked the Major. "No, Major! I know!" responded Sam. Then, the Major said, "You know that thought that you have about your girl. You're good, because, if she was a he, she would not be still sitting in that car with you." The Major then added, "See you at the base," and hung up. "This whole day has been so weird!" Sam thought to himself, and then looked up at the black helicopter hovering overhead, and watched as it sped off.

The evening was approaching fast, and, given all the distractions that had taken place over the previous 48 hours or so, Tony decided to go ahead with his party. Everyone turned out except the filthy rich like Oprah, who usually knew the important news before it became mainstream news, but the Donald must have been out of the country because he showed up, got updated on what had happened, and left immediately. But, there were still TV and movie celebrities, and star football players. The media had long loved Tony; he had charmed the gay world by showing other gays how powerful you could become, and tonight Tony was going to announce to his guests that he was performing a union for seven couples for a handsome price tag of two million dollars per couple.

The evening got off to a great start for everyone, especially for Tony. He was greeting his guests when a question was raised about why police were at his home a few hours earlier. Tony smiled and said, "They were looking for a missing cat, and my bodyguards escorted it out!"

In came some of the biggest names in Hollywood and a host of dignitaries from around the world, including ambassadors from twenty different countries who came to witness the extravaganza. But Puggley was pissed, and called Sam back to vent to him. Sam's phone rang eight times before his voicemail picked up. "Sam, I know you hear your phone ringing," said Puggley, adding, "You're probably laid up in a hotel with that pretty little April! And that's not fair at all!" shouted Puggley. "You – laid up, Tony having a party bigger than the President's Ball, and I've got to drive all the way back down there by myself. Somebody needs to tell me what the hell is going on!" said Puggley. He then redialed Sam's number, and, as before, the phone rang eight times, and Sam's voicemail picked up. "You might just as well answer," said Puggley, adding,

"I'm going to just keep calling back until you do." So, once again, he hung up and called right back. This time it went straight to voice mail because, after the second call, April had reached over and turned the phone off. She wanted no more distractions It had taken her fifteen years to decide to be with a man in an intimate way after her father's abuse, and she made that very clear to Sam when she said to him, "Please be gentle with me. I have never been with another man since my dad," said April with tears in her eyes. "We don't have to do this if you don't want to," said Sam, wiping the tears from her cheeks. "No, I want to," said April, "And I want to do it with you!" with breaks in her voice. Sam, being the gentleman that he was, asked her yet once again, "Are you sure?" "I was sure the first time I talked to you. I've waited all my adult life for a man that I could love and allow him to make love to me. After our first conversation, I knew you were 'the one,'" said April, as she leaned over and kissed Sam's lips with her very soft and moist lips. Sam responded by putting his arms around her and pulling her in tight, but not too tight. The two lay across the bed, passionately kissing and holding each other. Then, Sam gracefully eased her blouse off, revealing her beautiful, full breasts, and nipples that were pointing slightly upward – in full bloom. After a few more deep kisses on her mouth, Sam began to work his way down to her voluptuous breasts. From the left to the right, Sam gently kissed both breasts and nipples passionately, and licked and sucked her nipples in a tender, loving manner. April slowly closed her eyes and moaned with excitement, pleasure, and passion as Sam slowly made his way back up, past her slender shoulders and neck, and, finally, again gently planted kisses on her beautiful, moist lips. They then slowly – yet eagerly – undressed each other, and, once again, Sam asked, "Are you. . ." But, before he could complete his question, April pulled him in close and kissed him passionately. Sam then reached over to turn out the lights. . .

But, as the lights were going out in their bedroom, the ones in Baltimore were just coming on.

Chapter 7

Putting the Puzzle Pieces Together

Puggley was about to get into his car when Antoine pulled up beside him. "What's up, Puggs?" asked Antoine. "Just chilling," said Puggley, adding, "Yeah. About to head back south. Damn!!!" "That sucks," said Antoine. Then he added, "Man, Tony is having the party of a lifetime! DAMN!!! That's the same thing I told Sam." Said Puggley "You've talked to Sam?" asked Antoine. "Well, not really. I kind of left him a message, but I was saying the same thing," explained Puggley. "Where is Sam?" asked Antoine. "I don't know," replied Puggley, then adding, "I've got to go. I'll see you next time!" Puggley turned the music up and put the car in reverse. As soon as he backed out, another car zoomed in beside Antoine. "You in a big hurry, huh!" said Puggley, looking at the driver – after which he took a deep breath and said, "Jackass."

When he was about a block away, Puggley remembered that this was his stop and he had been to get a coffee for the road; so, he quickly pulled over. He had been thrown off by Antoine asking about Sam. As Puggley looked in the rearview mirror, he heard a certain sound simultaneously with seeing it; it was rapid gunfire, and Antoine, sitting in his car, was the intended target. Puggley, now rapidly trying to make a U-turn, bumped into two cars, and, before he could get there, the gunmen hurriedly sped off. Antoine must have taken about fifteen bullets, but, surprisingly, was still alive – but barely. "Who was it, 'toine?" asked Puggley. "Who did this, man?" Antoine could hardly speak, due to the internal bleeding that he was now beginning to cough up, but through the thickness of the blood in his throat, he squeezed Puggley's hand and said, "Look out for Tony." "Tell me who did this to you?"

asked Puggley again, as he dialed 911. "He's the one who killed Sal," said Antoine. "Who, Antoine? Who killed Sal?" asked Puggley. "Tell the Major that he was right; look out for Tony!" replied Antoine, gasping for air. "Tell me! Who did this!" asked Puggley again. "It was Freddie," whispered Antoine. "I need an ambulance!" shouted Puggley at the 911 operator, adding, "My brother has been shot multiple times." As he began to give them the address, a store manager came out yelling, "I called the police!" And, as he was speaking, the sounds of sirens fast approaching were evident. "Hold on 'toine! Just hold on," Puggley kept saying. He then added, "The medic is almost here! Just hold on!" Antoine took one short breath and said, "Freddie." "I heard you, but don't try to talk and don't worry; I'm going to get that son of a bitch!" As the ambulance pulled up, Antoine raised his eyes for the last time, and, in a dying plea, said, "Please look out for my little brother Tony." Puggley hesitated for a second, and then said, "I will, I will." he said once again, but Antoine was dead. A tear rolled down Puggley's face as the paramedics began to work on Antoine. "I can't get a pulse! let's get him into the ambo!" said one of the medics.

Puggley then got to his feet, and headed inside the store. While the officer was questioning the store manager, Puggley walked in and interrupted, "Did you get a look at those guys?" Before the manager could answer, Puggley asked further, "Have they ever been here before?" "Yeah. I believe they have," said the manager. "Where do you keep your recorder?" asked Puggley. "In the back office," answered the manager. "Lead the way," said Puggley. "Hold on, sir," said the police officer. "It's okay," said Puggley, practically pushing the manager toward the back. "Are you a police officer?" asked the lady cop. "Yeah. Something like that," answered Puggley, as they approached the back office. When the manager opened the door, Puggley pushed his way forward with such force that his fake beard became twisted. The lady police officer, noticing it immediately, tapped the store manager on the back, and nodded for him to step aside. She slowly pulled her service weapon and said, "Sir, I need for you to put both hands on top of your head, and slowly stand up." Puggley turned and looked at her as he was retrieving the disc, saying, "No disrespect to you, ma'am; but this disc is going with me." Before he could finish his sentence, she called for backup from the dozens of officers who had swarmed the store. Eight of them charged into the back room. By then, Puggley was on his feet and about to go into a self defense mode when the special ring tone came through his phone that was hanging on his belt. Puggley pulled his shirt up, turned completely around, and said, "My phone! I've got to get that!" When he answered, he started by saying, "They killed Antoine." "Let them take you, Puggley." "Take me where, Major? I know who did it," said Puggley. "So do we, so let them take you; don't lose your cool. You know the procedure: give them something, but give them nothing. I'll be there in a couple of hours. And, Puggley, I mean it! Let them take you! I'm heading to the air strip as we speak. Have you talked to Sam yet?" asked the Major. "No," answered Puggley, slowly. "Then don't tell him," said Major Travis. Puggley hung up his phone, put it in sleep mode, turned it off, and put it in his shirt pocket. "Who were you just talking to?" asked the female officer, as she placed cuffs on Puggley. "My mother!"responded Puggley, angrily. "Do you always call your mother 'major?'" she asked. "Yeah. My dad say it makes her feel like she is in charge," responded Puggley, further adding, "Would you like for me to call you major, also." The female officer began to go through his pockets, taking all of his possessions, including his wallet, his phone, and about $600.00 in cash. As she placed his items in a bag, Puggley realized that his military ID was in his wallet – placed there in anticipation of his return to base. So he burst out, "What kind of shit is this?!" And, "What are you charging me with?" he asked. "Obstruction, with the intent to steal evidence, for starters, and failure to respond to the command of a uniformed police officer," she replied. "Maybe you gave me the wrong command," said Puggley. "Oh yeah? And what command should that have been?" she asked, as she tightened the cuffs. "Hey!" said Puggley; he was about to answer her when a six foot ten inch, 300 pound uniformed hard stripe sergeant walked in. Puggley looked up at him briefly, but then turned back to the female officer and said, "If you had said, 'let me put these cuffs on you,' and had taken me in the back room and done me like you do in your dreams at night. . ." said Puggley, first pausing, then adding, "I've heard about you lady cops. You guys have the same fantasies as the male cops." "You have. . ." Puggley was about to say, but was interrupted by the giant police sergeant. "Let's go!" he said, taking Puggley by the cuffs. "Is this his shit?" the big man asked. "Yes," responded the female officer; "but he's my collar." "Then do the report; but he's going with me. They want him down at Central District for questioning," said the big man; he then took Puggley outside, almost dragging him. "Get in the car," said the officer, opening the back door. Puggley hesitated for a moment, and even thought about taking the big man down; but then, he thought about the Major's orders. And, just when he was about to get in, the huge officer said, "'Please,'" but in a much softer voice. Puggley paused, looked at him briefly, and then glanced at Antoine's dead body lying on the gurney, and his blood that had soaked through the white sheets that covered him. Puggley then looked left and right, and then slowly got into the car. The officer quickly closed the door, and walked around to the driver's seat; but, for the six seconds that it took him to get to that door, Puggley picked the lock on the cuffs – waiting for his opportunity to escape.

There were too many friends dying around him, and he no longer trusted his commanding officer. He sat in the back of the patrol car planning his escape; after a four-block ride, the officer stopped the car and began talking on his cell. "Come on around. He's in the back seat," said the officer. Puggley's mind began to race as bright lights approached from the rear. The officer got out, and went back to meet the person getting out of the car. Both persons then walked up to the car in which Puggley was located. Puggley dug into the back seat in a crouching position, with his mind made up to strike by leaping through the window after their first shot shred the window; but, instead of shooting through the window, they just opened the door. "This is even better," thought Puggley. And, just as he took his last look at the two advancing men, and before striking, he noticed that the first man who was walking to the patrol car was Tony. "What the f--k?" thought Puggley.

Tony opened the door and said, "Come on, Puggley. I already know." Puggley paused and was about to reply when the officer said "Let me take those cuffs off." Puggley handed the cuffs to the officer and followed Tony. "What the hell is going on?" asked Puggley. "I don't know," replied Tony, "but I do know that they killed my cousin, and now my brother." With tears running down both sides of his face, Tony added, "Them motherf---ers killed my brothers, and that major guy had something to do with it!" Puggley listened carefully because he, too, had suspicions of Major Travis. "Are you talking about my major, Major Travis?" asked Puggley. "If that's his name." Then, suddenly, the van they were sitting in almost sank to the ground when the large cop got in; just that quick, he had changed clothes. Tony hurried and pulled off, leaving the police car there.

"I have to call Sam," said Puggley. "I already did," interrupted Tony. "How did you get through?" asked Puggley. "April called me. She told me how your major friend pulled them over and strip searched her." "That crazy major wouldn't do anything like that," said Puggley, while taking his personal belonging from the would-be cop. "I take it you're not a real cop." Said Puggley. The big man smiled and said, "No. But I've played one on television before." "Sam should be there by the time we get home," said Tony. "Be where?" asked Puggley. "At my house. A friend of mine is flying him up to BWIMarshall Airport in his private plane, and I'm having my private helicopter fly him to my house," responded Tony. "You have a helicopter?" Puggley asked. "I have a private Jet, too, but I grounded the crew until they re-wax it and put some Armor all on all those tires." Tony continued, "They're talking about the possibility that it might make the plane's brakes drag. Have you ever heard of such foolishness?" asked Tony. But Puggley couldn't respond because he was still thinking about Tony's plane and helicopter; then, he finally replied, "Let me get this shit straight.

You mean you have that big ass house, all of those cars, a hundred-foot boat. . ." "A yacht," corrected Tony. ". . . a helicopter, and a private jet, and you got all that shit through a gay dating service?" asked Puggley. "Never underestimate the power of gay people," said Tony with a smile as he drove down the highway. "Why was Antoine in Baltimore?" Puggley asked Tony. "I don't know." "He said he had to take care of something at the club, but you don't know what it was?" asked Puggley. "No. He wouldn't tell me," responded Tony. "But I know he was seeing that floozy Delilah, or whatever she calls herself. As a matter of fact, I'm gonna tell them to cut that bitch's throat," said Tony, dialing his phone. "Whoa! Whoa!" said Puggley, snatching the phone out of Tony's hand, adding, "You can't do that. If you kill her, we can't question her." "Then I'll just tell them to lock that bitch in the basement until we come back," said Tony, reaching his hand out for his phone. But Puggley said, "No, Tony. I can't let you do that either," then explaining, "She can't be in this alone." "You're damn right!" said Tony, interrupting Puggley, "Because I know that that major friend of yours is involved." "Well, we won't know anything unless you do it my way, and when we get to your house, we'll run it past Sam; but, right now, this is what we're going to do. You are going to call your friends and have them just keep a close eye on her and follow her wherever she goes, or have some of your cop friends watch her," said Puggley, still holding onto Tony's cell phone. "Yes, you're right, Puggley. I also want to question that bisexual bitch," added Tony. "Bisexual?" asked Puggley. "Yeah. That bitch has licked more pussy than a cat's meow, but I think 'twoine liked watching that shit. I never trusted them bisexuals," said Tony, pulling the van into a gas station. As soon as he stopped, the big man got out, and, in a tiny voice, said, "Don't forget about later on tonight." Tony smiled, gave him a sexy, playful wink, and said, "Bye, Tiny." The big man blew Tony a kiss as Puggley hurriedly leaned back out of their communication track. "Now, is Big twice the size of Hulk Hogan, guy gay?" asked Puggley. "Yes, he is, and he loves some of me." "You know that I'm not gay, so when I say that's a big man, Tony. . ." "Yes, I know,"he responded, "But he's a fem." "What?" asked Puggley. "Why do you think they call him Tiny, but where it fits in the back, it's deep and cut, cut, cut." "I get the picture," said Puggley, then asking, "Tell me something; how can you say that you don't like bisexuals, yet, you go both ways yourself?" "That's a lie!" snapped Tony. "I'm strictly dickley." "Not if you're going up in that big man's butt," Puggley said. "But he's not a woman," Tony responded, "so that's just being 100% gay." "No!" Puggley responded. "No! That's just 100% nasty!" as he leaned his head against the window to take a nap for the rest of the ride.

But, as he slept, the Major was wide awake, and homing in on both Puggley and Sam, thanks to the microchip implants that had been placed beneath their skin when they first entered the training program. Puggley tossed and turned in the front seat, trying to sleep. Tony suggested that he to lay down on the back seat in the van, but Puggley, being homophobic, and worrying about someone seeing him, declined; given all that had just happened in such a short period of time, he just had had too much on his mind to sleep, so he put his head phones on, tilted his head back, closed his eyes, and rested. A little further south, the Major was in a rapid mode to get to Baltimore.

"Be careful with that lap top," said the Major as he boarded the C130 north-bound to Andrews Air Force Base. The Major knew everything that had happened; he even knew where both Puggley and Sam were through the computer chip tracking device implanted under their skin. Sparky and J.J. accompanied the Major, while two other agents headed toward Sam's location. The Major knew that Sam had left, but he was not about to tell that to the two agents because they were from another unit. By the time they reached the motel, Sam had landed at Thurgood Marshall B.W.I., and had taken off in Tony's helicopter – heading for Southern Maryland. But, the sky was full of flyers – all heading in the same direction; that is, to Baltimore.

Freddie and his four-man protection crew were also heading to Baltimore. The Major and the joint agencies were tracking all movements of Freddie and all persons associated with him; so, when a flight left B.W.I. with persons known to be affiliated with Freddie's organization, and with a destination of Atlanta, red flags were raised because they knew that he had invested in a club there. But the flags were raised too late because Freddie had stopped short at a private air strip just outside of Washington, D.C. He had gotten off the private jet, and onto a helicopter. Because he knew they would be waiting for him in Atlanta, he had his pilot fly him back to Baltimore.

As Major Travis's C130 came to its final approach, his cell phone went into a special ring tone. "Travis," he said, answering the phone while walking to the rear of the plane. "Abort, Major!" said the person on the other end. "What?" Major Travis responded. "You heard me, Major," said the other person, adding, "Ron, they are picking your team off one by one; your whole crew has been compromised, and we can't afford to lose another Marine with no results." "But, General," said Major Travis, "that's the whole point! This son of a bitch has killed not only four members from my team, but he has also killed a good friend of both of ours, and I'm within a day of catching this bastard. I'm too close, General. You can't pull me off now!" "At what cost?!" the General shouted back, "You've chased this piece of shit all over the Middle East and the Far East. You lost him in Hong Kong, and you said that you had him here in the U.S." "And he's still here," interrupted the Major. "Well, that's irrelevant to you now," said the General. "The orders came down from the Pentagon; it's CIA's problem now." "What?" Major Travis protested. "He's here; he's not on foreign soil. How could you let them do that?" "That may be true, but he's an international criminal, and I didn't let them do anything! You've been a Marine long enough to know how the game is played, Major." "Sir, all I'm saying is that I've got him on the run like a rat, and pretty soon he's going to run out of holes to hide in," added the Major. "Major Travis, all of that sounds good, but it's out of my hands," said the General, then adding, "You got your promotion, Ron, to full colonel and base commander at Parris Island, and you were chosen over two brigadier generals. It sets you up for promotion within a year to general; it's Uncle Sam's way of thanking you for your loyal services through the years. Now, I need you to pack it up and bring everything that you have on him to the briefing on Monday so they can take the ball and run." "So, no matter what I say, come Monday, I have to turn everything over to them?" asked the Major.

"That's affirmative!" the General responded. "So that gives me 48 hours to nab this m----rf-- --r," the Major added. "Damn it, Ron! This is why you were passed over for promotion the last three times – because of your renegade behavior. You had your chance. He has managed to smuggle forty more operatives into the U.S., and, although we know the location of each of them, we must bring him down first. We can't allow this guy to continue to operate," said the general. "I know what you're thinking, Ron, but, if it backfires and you lose another Marine, you can kiss it all goodbye – retirement, promotion, and maybe do some jail time. Do you really want to risk all of that?" he asked. But the Major only responded by saying, "I'll see you on Monday, sir."

The Major strapped himself in his seat as the plane began to land. "Where are they?" he shouted to Sparky. "The two are together, sir; it looks like they are heading back to Baltimore. They are currently heading north on route 301," responded Sparky. "Okay. When this plane stops, I want this gear in the vans pronto! You understand?" asked the Major. "Yes, Major, we understand!" both men replied. "And I'm not so sure that this cousin Tony is as innocent as he makes himself out to be," the Major added. "I tailed him for a week, Major, and found nothing. If he were white, he would be Mr. Clean. Outside of his perverted behaviors, he's just the dumb vessel that they are using to smuggle terrorist into the country." "Well, I'm not buying that dumb bit just because he managed to stay under the radar legally with the I.R.S.," said the Major, adding, "That S.O.B. is worth at least 1.5 billion easy; nobody gets that rich in that short period of time without doing something illegal." "But, we have Antoine's reports and Sal's," said J.J. "Well, both of them are dead, aren't they?" asked the Major. "Well, maybe if you had let Sal just ask him like he wanted. . ." "Whoa, whoa," said the Major, cutting him off.

"If I had allowed Sal to question Tony, the gig would have been up a long time ago because Tony would have run his mouth." "I don't know, Major. He and Sal were pretty close," said Stoney. "So, what are you two saying? It's my fault that they got killed?" the Major asked. "No, sir," Stoney responded. "Me, either, sir," added J.J. "I just know that it was no secret that Sal was close to Tony." "Yeah, too close," said the Major. As the two looked at each other, the plane landed and they began to unpack. While they unpacked, Sam and Puggley stocked up on weapons and ammo as if they were going to war (and, in their minds, they were). They didn't talk about Antoine or Sam because they now were in the past. Furthermore, this operation was not just about revenge; rather, this was the reckoning to destroy and break the backs of the organization and of all those who were involved in the slaying of Sal and Antoine.

Tony had connections to the underground world that were unbelievable.

They stopped in Cherry Hill and met a gay guy named Vincent, who got into the van with them as they drove to a small shopping mall. A security guard came out, walked over to the van, and spoke to Tony; then he opened the back garage door. When they first drove in, it was dark, and no lights were on other than the headlights of the van; but, within seconds, the flood lights came on, illuminating the entire inside. Tony jumped out and said "Come on!" But both Puggley and Sam proceeded with caution as they exited the van. Tony headed straight to the door that had an "Office" sign hanging over it; Puggley and Sam followed carefully with their hands on their weapons. Vincent followed in second place behind Tony. When Sam walked in, he immediately recognized one of the guys, Leroy, an old childhood friend of the three of them. Leroy owned a tow truck business on paper, but, in fact, he was one of the largest illegal gun dealers on the East Coast! "Leroy!" said Sam when he first saw him. "Yeah! It's me! What's up, Puggley?" he asked. "I'm cool," responded Puggley, adding, "What up with you?" "Chilling, chilling," answered Leroy saying further, "That's some wicked shit that happened to Antoine and Sal, but I have everything you need to smoke those m----rf----rs." Puggley and Sam were stocking up on everything when the out-front look-out man came running in, shouting, "Feds! Feds! Feds!" They all quickly scrambled to take defensive positions, when Major Travis walked in, saying, "Just what the hell do you guys think you are doing?" Sam and Puggley both were surprised by the Major's arrival.

"So, you guys decided to take matters into your own hands," said the Major as Stoney and J.J. stood beside him with their weapons pointing at them. "You guys are not going to do this by yourself. We've been ordered to stand down," said the Major. All four team members looked at each other as the Major added, "But we are not going to stand down – at least not until we capture or kill that S.O.B. Freddie; and we have until Monday to do that." But Tony, still suspicious of Major Travis, bucked on his every word, and said, "How the hell do we know that we can trust you?" as his hand continued to strongly clinch his gun. "How the hell do we know we can trust you? I mean, after all, you and Freddie are butt buddies, I mean best buddies," said the Major, sarcastically. "Freddie? She's just a business associate," said Tony. "That's bullshit!" said Major Travis. "Number one, she's a he, and, number two, he financed your club." "Wrong!" said Tony. "He helped finance me, and that's because I arranged weddings for him and his friends from around the world. And, yeah, I got paid good for it." "No, you got paid for smuggling terrorists into the country," said Major Travis, "and allowing them motherf----rs to kill your brother and your cousin." Those words cut through Tony like a knife. He drew his pistol, but Sam quickly grabbed Tony's hand and got between the two. "At this point, Major, I want to shoot you myself," said Sam, "but I need to know what's going on myself." "Yeah, Major! There's been some real weird shit going on lately," said Puggley. "It's all been on a needto-know basis, and, up until now, you guys did not need to know; but the time has come to tell you the real deal," said the Major. "Tony, you and your guys leave out for a minute," requested Sam. "No, they don't have to. I wasn't joking when I said that the General has scrapped the mission and turned it over to the CIA. We are going to need all the help we can get, and I believe you know where he is," said the Major. "I know he's still here in Baltimore, and if I thought that he had anything to do with killing my brother and cousin, I would kill him myself," said Sam. "Well, he did," said Major Travis as he began to tell them the operation of the mission, and the roles that Sal and Antoine had played.

CHAPTER 8
The Big Picture

"We have been after this bastard for over fifteen years now," the Major explained. "That's more than half of some of you guys' lives. He has managed to cleverly elude just about every law enforcement division around the world, and mainly because of guys like you, Tony." "What the hell do you mean by 'guys like me'?" Tony snapped back. "Oh, I don't mean you in general. I mean gay people." "Now you want to bash gays, huh, Mr. Major?" responded Tony angrily. "No. What I'm saying is," said the Major before he was interrupted by Tony saying, "Go ahead and say it, Mr. motherf----r." "If you'd let me finish, I will," replied the Major. "Chill out, Tony," said Sam, adding, "We all need to hear this."

"Well, as I was saying, he puts on a gay front. He may perform gay acts, but you have to be human to be gay, and, with all the inhumane things that this piece of shit has done, you can hardly call him human. He has blown up more U.S. embassies, or had a hand in making it happen – more than any other terrorist in the world; and he has been paid very well for his involvements," said the Major. "Well, I know that he's not a true gay," said Tony, adding, "He's a f g bisexual." "Yo, Tony! Can you shut the hell up!" interrupted Puggley, adding, "You can hit on the Major later." "F--k you, Puggley," Tony snapped back; "you must want your ass whipped again." "Don't flatter yourself," said Puggley, adding, "That was a long time ago." He then looked intensely at Tony and said, "Hey, Tony. Why don't you either wait until the Major finishes, or wait outside?" Sam calmly replied, "I'm going to keep quiet." "But don't you say anything to me," mumbled Tony.

The Major began to tell the saga once again. "What Freddie does is play on the sympathy of real gay people, and, in this case, you Tony! He fronted you the money to get your business and his business off the ground. Your business is totally legit – International Gay Marriage, Inc. He has sent over forty-nine sleepers into the United States posing as gay couples. We know where all of them are, except the ones that just came into the country yesterday to attend your party. We knew where they were, thanks to Sal. That's why they had him killed, and made it look like it was gang related. Freddie ordered the hit. And Antoine confirmed it through an informer from his organization, so that's why they killed him; he was putting ALL of the pieces together: He had just made a positive ID on Freddie, and, furthermore, the informer had told him about ALL of Freddie's usual hiding places; but, tonight, he was going to reveal the final and most important and most secluded hiding place that Freddie retreats to when he's on the run. "He was here tonight," said Tony, with tears instantly streaming prolifically from his eyes. "He asked me not to tell anyone because he doesn't like publicity; but, he asked me where was Antoine, and I told him," said Tony, crying loudly. "I f g helped kill my own dear brother! Oh my God!" screamed Tony at the top of his lungs, dropping his face into the palm of his hands. "Don't blame yourself," counseled Major Travis. "This ruthless son of a bitch killed his own son at the dinner table, and sat there and finished his dinner while his son bled out."
Just then, the Major's phone rang.

"What? When? I figured as much," said the Major, speaking to the other person on the line. "I'm briefing my team as we speak. Yes. Right," said the Major, still on the phone. "No. You guys stay in place. I'll worry about that on Monday," said the Major, hanging up and then turning to his team. "I figured as much. That was the D.E.A. in Atlanta. His plane landed there, but Freddie wasn't on it.

That rat is running out of holes," said the Major, adding, "I had him cornered in Hong Kong, and he pulled the same disappearing act on us there. He faked as if he had gotten on a helicopter heading across the bay toward Kaloon; Chinese military helicopters forced him to land. But, when they approached the chopper, he wasn't in it – just the pilot and a relative of his; and, after standing by the helicopter for about two minutes – questioning the pilot and checking for trap doors that he could be hiding behind, the chopper blew up, killing three Chinese military officers, two U.S. Marines who were on detachment like us, plus his own men. The bomb had been set to detonate upon the landing of the helicopter so that no one could count the bodies; but something went wrong, and it went off too late. If it had been any later, I wouldn't be here today; but I traded places with a good friend of mine because he wanted to see the Kaloon side of Hong Kong. My chopper was landing when Freddie's 'copter exploded. Freddie blamed it on the Chinese government and hid among the underground Chinese gay community – almost causing a riot in Tenemen Square. But it wasn't until we flew back to the other roof top that I noticed the trap door on top of the building. I pointed it out to a first lieutenant, who was third in command; but nobody listened, and Freddie got away. However, this time we are on American soil, and I'm counting on you and your friends to help me corner this rat for good," said the Major, looking at Tony. "Now, that was nice work that you did on those kids who killed Sal, but this one has to be kept alive." "It was Freddie who told me where that kid was," said Tony, looking down.

"He had you kill them so that they could never tell on him," the Major replied. "He's very cunning and manipulative; but, with the help of your people, we can get him. And, I mean get him tonight!" said the Major, repeating, "But we have to have him alive in case some of his sleepers have gotten through without us noticing them." "What do you want me to do?" asked Tony. "Here," said the Major, handing him pictures of Freddie in different disguises. "I'm sure he has more, but these are his favorites, or they are what we have seen him in most recently. Now, I know you might think you know this man, Tony, but you really don't. This man is a cold hearted killer. It's rumored that he killed his own mother for her condemning him for being gay," said the Major, adding, "If any of your people see him, call Sam immediately!"

Within minutes, about fifty of Tony's friends were out back with almost as much fire power as the Major's team. They were almost like a Frankenstein mob – a mixture of uniformed Baltimore City cops, several fire chiefs, ministers, and professionals in their uniforms: nurses, security guards, McDonalds workers, other fast food chain workers, etc. Tony turned, looked at Sam, and addressed the whole team. "If he's out there, we'll find him." The Major then added, "Let's hope so," and began to instruct his team. Then, Tony turned again and said, "Never under-estimate the power of gay," as he left the building.

As they began their search for Freddie, hours passed, but Freddie was nowhere to be found. Tony even skipped his party, and, with the help of his friends at the Baltimore City Police Department, was able to keep his club open until four in the morning in hopes that Freddie would go there; but, no such luck materialized. About three o'clock Sunday afternoon, Tony called Sam. "I can't say for sure, but I think we might have found his murdering ass." "Where?" asked Sam. "I could find out for sure if your asshole boss weren't such an ass," said Tony. "Where, Tony?" asked Sam, ignoring Tony's sarcasm. "Bring your dead ass team upstairs and I'll show you." Sam walked over to the Major, who was sleeping on the couch, gave him a little shake, and said, "Major, Tony thinks they may have found him." The Major shot up to an upright sitting position. The Major was wide eyed and fully alert. Stoney and Puggley jumped up from their table and followed the Major.

When they reached Tony's office, a Deputy Chief from the Central District was explaining where they believed Freddie was. "There's a night club in the center of the 2200 Block of Maryland Avenue. As one of our cars drove by, the officer noticed a slight disturbance between several individuals. Our officer described four persons – two females, who appeared to be protecting a third person described as an older male dressed in drag." "And the fourth person?" asked the Major; but the Deputy Chief was taking a quick look at Puggley's butt while Puggley was leaning over, tying his boots. "The fourth man?" the Major asked again. "Oh yeah," the Deputy Chief said, clearing his throat and turning his attention back to the Major. "We have a picture of him," he said, as he began to show them the recording from the officer's dash cam. "Well, I'll be damned!" said the Major, further asking, "Where is the SOB now?" The Deputy Chief called on his cell, spoke for a moment, and then hung up; he then turned to Tony and the Major, saying, "He's in a club at North Avenue and Howard Street." "I know the owner of that club," said Tony, adding, "I'll have some of my friends hold him until we get there." "Whoa!!!" said all four team members simultaneously, looking at each other. "No," said the Major. "His nephew Paul is very dangerous. He's killed over fifteen men, ten of them with his bare hands. No. I would prefer that you have a couple of your uniformed officers pick him up and detain him until we get there." Looking at his men, the Major warned, "He holds five grand master belts in five different martial arts. You don't want to rub him the wrong way. You can question him about the incident that happened outside of the other club; but don't scare this guy because you don't know who Freddie may have there watching out for him." "We're the ones who found them, we should be able to do something," said Tony, feeling left out. "You can do something," said the Major. "Have one of your friends drive by the scene with their radio blasting as loud as possible. That will allow your people to ask him to get into the car, and explain to him that getting into the car would mean that he would have to be handcuffed temporarily." "Well, if he's that bad, cuffs are not going to do any good," said Tony. "That's right! It won't!" the Major replied, adding, "But, if he does go nuts, it'll slow him down until we get there," said the Major as he headed out with his team. "Ain't that a bitch!" Tony mumbled, as he raced to do the opposite of what the Major had asked.

So, as the Major and his team headed toward Freddie's nephew Paul, Tony and four of his friends, strapped up with mini submachine guns, jumped on their high speed motorcycles, and headed aggressively toward Freddie. As the Major briefed his crew en route, he continued to express, "We need both him and Freddie alive!" When they pulled up to the club, the Major handed Sam a stun gun, saying, "Don't miss or we'll have to kill him. And be sure to call your cousin, and tell him to have his officers' roll down both rear windows simultaneously, and we'll take it from there."

"Hello! Tony?" asked Sam. "No!" the person at the other end said. "This is Deputy Chief Jones." "Where's Tony?" asked Sam. "He left," said the Deputy Chief. "Left to go where?" asked Sam. "He's headed to Maryland Avenue – where the other guy is." "Shit! Shit" said Sam as he hung up. The Major looked at Sam as they were getting out of their car, and said, "Don't tell me that that damn fool cousin of yours has gone after Freddie." "Yeah! Major! That's exactly what he's done," replied Sam. "Puggley and Stoney, get over there right now! It's just around the corner!" "I know where it is," said Puggley as he walked around to the driver's side and almost got hit by a group of four motorcycles that were speeding past. "Don't go in. Just cover the front and back, and remember two things: One, he's a master of disguise, and two, we need him alive! Got it, Puggley?" asked the Major. "Yeah, Major! I got it!" replied Puggley as he got behind the wheel. Puggley then looked at the Major and asked, "Are you guys going to be alright?" "Get out of here!" said the Major, as he and Sam waited for the windows to come down; when the windows did come down, they approached the car at the same time.

"Hey! Paul!" said the Major as Sam tazed him. As he turned toward the Major, Paul asked, "Why did you do that?" adding, "I saw you when you first got out of your car. I wanted to tell you where he was, as well as his very flawed and dangerous character: He's crazy; he had drugged me, and handcuffed me to a bed, and had anal sex with me until I bled." "Yeah, I guess that's a pretty rotten thing for an uncle to do," said Sam, looking in the car. "Rotten! Rotten!, you say. I'm not f--k-- g gay." "Damn!" said the Major, adding, "Tell us where he is before you pass out." "He's in the club on Maryland Avenue, but he won't be in there because he will use a secret door that leads to the building next door, where he has a loft on the third floor," said Paul as he was about to pass out. "How many bodyguards?" asked the Major. "Don't know. Maybe ten that I trained," he said as he blinked out.

The Major looked at the Deputy Chief and said, "Get some back up, and keep those cuffs on him; and put some ankle chains on him as well, and don't take them off until I get there." He then looked at Paul and then at Sam, and pulled out a stun gun of his own and tazed Paul with his second "dose." The Major then said, "He really is a dangerous dude," as he walked over to an undercover police officer and said, "Let's go!" As they turned the corner, the Major was on his phone, asking, "Where's my back up?" as he put his phone on speaker. "Right behind you," the other person responded. "Okay. We've got a possible ten, or better, aggressive assailants inside – armed and extremely dangerous. All of them are masters of multiple martial arts; do not underestimate them because they happen to be gay men and women. These guys are vicious murderers."

"We're in place," said Puggley, breaking through on the twelve-way line that the Major was now communicating on. "Oh, yeah! Major. Tony and his friends beat us here; they're already inside." "Damn it!" said the Major. "This changes the game!" "No, Major," said Sam. "Tony and his guys can handle themselves pretty well!" "Yeah! That's the problem. I need Freddie alive, and I don't think that Tony feels the same way. Three of you go around to the back with Stoney. Then, give me two shooters on top of the roof across the street. Listen up, people! Broaden your scope to three houses up and three houses, down – front and rear exits. The rest of us are going through the front. Lock and load people!" said the Major.

As the Major and his crew were about to enter the front, Tony was making his way up to Freddie, when one of two female bodyguards came down the steps, looked at Tony, and said, "Why are you here?" "I need to see Freddie," said Tony. "How did you know he was here?" the female bodyguard asked. "He told me to meet him here," said Tony, looking suspicious to the bodyguard. "Wait. I'll see if he's awake," said the bodyguard as she turned slightly, as if heading back up the steps, and then back-kicked Tony in the chest, knocking him to the bottom of the steps. Then, the real fighting began. Tony and his four friends had on bright pink jackets with the words 'Tony's Crew' written on the back in diamond sparkles, which made them easier to recognize. "Alright!" said the Major. "Let's go in." "Hey, be careful!" said Sam to one of the other team members. "Shit! It's just a bunch of gays," said the six foot ten, two hundred sixty-pound man, smiling. On that note, the Major turned the door knob and opened the door.

Fighting was already in progress, with Tony and his crew kicking ass. They had spread out in a sweep with their ample weapons. Then, gunfire rang out. "Tony! Get your people out of here!" shouted Sam as return fire issued forth. The big agent ducked into the kitchen – looking for more targets. As he entered the rear of the kitchen, a small gay man in a cook's uniform greeted him, saying, "Can I help you?" The big agent looked at the little gay man and said, "Put your hands up over your head." The small man did just that, as femininely as he could. Just as the agent was about to cuff him, the small gay man jumped up and double kicked the big man in his chest, and then landed a spinning kick to the side of his head – sending him backwards. As the big man was about to hit the floor, the little man quickly grabbed a sharp kitchen knife, and headed toward the big agent laying on the floor. Just as he drew the knife back to stab him in the heart, shots rang out, with Sam pulling the trigger that dropped the cook to the floor. The big man looked over at Sam and dropped his head. "Come on, get up," said Sam, extending his hand, and helping him up. Just as the big man got to his feet, a bullet caught him in the side of his neck, sending him back to the floor, and pulling Sam down with him. Sam quickly turned his weapon toward the sound of empty casings dropping, and let off a rapid burst that brought the gunman to his knees; Sam then quickly finished him off with a bullet to the head.

"Are you alright?" asked Sam as he tended to the big man's wound, adding, "You're lucky; it went right through your neck and missed the jugular. I want you to stay here; I'm going to send one of Tony's guys in. Okay?" asked Sam as he grabbed another clean dish cloth; then, he reached into the agent's shirt pocket and pulled out a pack of cigarettes. "Matches are in the other pocket," said the big man, who then looked at Sam and asked, "I'm going to die, aren't I?" Sam just looked at him and dumped the cigarettes out onto the ground. "What the f--k!" said the agent; but, Sam took the plastic clear wrapping from the pack, placed it over the bullet wound, and covered it with a clean dish cloth. "Hold it there," said Sam, as he placed the agent's hand over the cloth. Then, standing up slowly and walking cautiously over to the dead shooter lying on the floor, Sam slowly opened the door to the dining room and was startled by one of Tony's guys in search of Tony. "Whoa!" said Sam as they confronted each other. "We can't find Tony," he said. Sam looked at him and said, "Stay with my friend here; we'll find Tony." Just then. Puggley walked in. "The Major is missing, too. I think they may have found a secret door; everyone else is rounding up the rest of them assholes who tried to run. Come on; it's got to be up here," said Puggley, leading the way up the steps. Little did he know that he was about to meet the same fate as the Major and Tony, but stopped when Sam heard a noise at the other end of the hall, and turned to head in that direction. When Sam reached the other end of the hallway, he realized that the noise was his team members and local police outside, loading Freddie's bodyguards into the transport vans, so he waved 'all clear' to Puggley, which set him in motion the other way; but Sam could see from a distance what Puggley couldn't see up close, which was toes sticking out the bottom of the curtain that Puggley was about to pass. Sam sent several bullets zooming past Puggley, who turned around and briefly pointed his weapon at Sam. Puggley then looked to his left and saw the body as it slumped down behind the curtain. When he pulled the curtain back, it revealed the hidden door covered with wall paper; a superficial viewing would not have allowed a casual viewer to find it. They moved the body to the side and carefully opened the door. Puggley went in first and took on fire. He got hit in the chest and in the leg; his bulletproof vest protected his chest, but the bullet that hit his leg put him down. There was nowhere to find cover, and the shooting was coming from a remote defense cam that fired 9mm rounds mounted on the wall. Sam shot at it in fully automatic mode, but was unable to hit it. Puggley then aimed his pistol and, with just one shot, took it out. Sam got to his feet and ran over to Puggley, and was about to kneel down when he was kicked in the face by a very beautiful, but familiar face. She kicked him so hard that he almost flipped backwards; but, instead, he fell back about ten feet. She rushed him, but Sam – thinking quickly, rolled to the side as she tried to chop him with the fire ax that she had grabbed off the wall. Sam managed to get to his feet, but she continued to whale the ax, with a few near misses. Sam had dropped his gun when she kicked him. Puggley was desperately trying to crawl toward an area where he could get a clear shot, but once she noticed what he was trying to do, she took a last swing at Sam and then back flipped, and stood directly over Puggley and raised the ax to chop his head off. Sam scrambled to get his weapon, but it was too late, because, by the time he retrieved his gun, the ax was in a downward trajectory as she said, "Say good night!" Then, shots rang out, and a voice followed. "Bitch, please!" said Tony after shooting her. "Where the hell did you come from?" asked Sam. "And, where is the Major?" "I don't know," said Tony, adding, "there must be another door or room." "I'll find it," said Sam, "but I need you, Tony, to go down and show them the way up here so they can get Puggley out of here before he bleeds to death.

Tony ran out screaming for help, while Sam pressed ahead, looking for Freddie and the Major. He was stopped by a brick wall that separated them from the next house. Looking at the wall, he noticed that some of the bricks were prefabricated and not connected to the other bricks. And, when he gave it a little push, it opened, revealing a disguised door. Sam eased his way forward as quietly as he could.

But, when he opened the door, Freddie said, "Come in, Sam, and join the party." Sam had never seen Freddie before, except in photos; but, Sam was not prepared for the image: Freddie was the creepiest man he had ever seen! He had facial features like a woman who had been battered all her life. His fingernails were two to three inches long, his face was caked with layers of makeup that only partially hid the stubble protruding from his neck. As Sam walked in, he also noticed the Major sitting and tied up in a chair, bleeding, and with a bomb strapped to his chest. He looked up at Sam and said, "Shoot this motherf----r." Sam took aim at Freddie, but Freddie just smiled and held the detonator up, saying, "Go ahead, Sammy! We all will go together." Sam paused and noticed that there were enough explosives attached to the Major to level the entire building, so he eased his weapon down, and Freddie's other female bodyguard came in from the ceiling with a submachine gun, blasting at Sam. He quickly tried to take cover and return fire. However, Freddie instructed the young lady to cease fire, saying, "I'm going to walk out of here with her, Sammy." "Don't let him go, Sam; shoot the bomb and the world will be a much better place. He killed your brother and your cousin," said the Major. "No!" shouted Freddie. "You killed them with your relentless pursuit of me! However, it's true that I never liked Sally, but only based on his name; on the other hand, I thought Antoine would have made an excellent warrior to be added to my army. But, no, he had to remain too loyal to you to the core, as he discussed with Tony."

The Major looked up at Sam at the same time that Sam's eyes met his. "Oh, don't look so surprised," said Freddie. "Antoine and my dear Tony are very close brothers; they always told each other everything, and I would just sit and listen; and that's how I've been able to escape from you these last few years. Now, do you think that I'm going to allow you jerks to destroy what has taken me years to build? I will offer to you what I offered your boss, Sammy," said Freddie. "If you join my team, I'll make you richer than you can ever imagine. Look at your cousin Tony's wealth. In just five minutes I can make you wealthy – worth millions – all around the world. All you have to do is put a bullet in his head and leave with us. You can take Tony's place; his fame and wealth will be yours. "I don't think so," said Sam, noticing Tony and one of his guys standing behind the door. But Sam needed a distraction so they could come in without taking fire; then, just as he was contemplating his next move, a spinning martial arts star zoomed past his head and struck the bodyguard in the arm, causing her to drop her weapon from her right hand. Tony rushed in with one of his crew, but she quickly drew another pistol from a leg holster and fired several shots, one of which hit Sam in the shoulder; but, before she could get off a fourth shot, Tony's man was all over her.

While Freddie tried to make his escape, the two put on a dazzling display of martial arts – blow for blow, and kick for kick. It was a fight that looked almost choreographed. It was not until Freddie's bodyguard was knocked to the ground, and the person fighting her pulled off her own scarf, that Sam realized that, not only was it a woman, but it was April; and she had royally kicked her ass. Tony ran behind Freddie and fired a single shot, hitting him in the lower back. Freddie dropped to the floor and looked back at Tony, saying, "I made you!" "No! God made me!" replied Tony as he walked slowly over to Freddie. "I gave you millions," said Freddie. "Yeah, but you killed my brother and my cousin; and you made me believe that it was someone else." "I had to," said Freddie. "It was for the good of the organization; besides, it was the Major who killed them." As Freddie lay there, holding the detonator, he looked up at Tony and added, "If I take my finger off this button, we all die." "Bullshit!" said Tony, with tears running through his mascara. "You killed my brother, you bisexual bitch!" as he shot him again – this time in the leg, which caused him to drop the detonator; then he added, "You killed my cousin," as he shot him again, in the other leg.

By now, the final countdown on the bomb's timer had begun – the timer being at a minute and thirty seconds. "Tony, I loved you," said Freddie, reaching for a gun under his shirt. Tony, still crying, unloaded ten bullets into Freddie's body before he walked away and headed back into the room where the Major and the others were, Sam frantically tried to disarm and discard the bomb that was strapped to Major Travis. April had beaten his bodyguard to a pulp, and now, she joined Sam to try to cut the bomb off the Major. "You guys get out of here, Sam," said the Major. "We've still got a minute," said Sam. "Get out of here! That's an order!" shouted the Major. Tony casually walked over to the Major and dropped the detonator in his lap. "Get out of here, Tony," said Sam, "and take April with you." "All of you, get the hell out of here!" barked the Major.

"Shut up, you old fart! They're trying to save your life." The bomb's timer was now down to fifteen seconds. "Get the hell out of here!" screamed the Major. "No!" said Tony, "we all go together." Sam looked at Tony as the bomb's timer hit the final five-second mark. Tony reached down and cut the belt off the Major just as the timer hit zero, but nothing happened. Tony threw the belt across the room and said, "Let's go!" "What the hell? How did you know the bomb wouldn't go off?" asked Sam. "Please! That self-centered SOB would never put himself in a dangerous situation. Plus, his nephew Paul called me right after y'all left, and told me," said Tony. Sam looked at Tony, and Tony looked at the Major, smiled, and said, "Never underestimate the power of gay people." The Major smiled and said, "Never again!"

Weeks went by, and things were almost back to normal. April and Sam were at the stop light at Pennsylvania and North Avenues in Baltimore when four young men crossed in front of them with their pants hanging off their exposed butts. They looked at April and remembered her from the severe hurt'n' she had put on them before. All four immediately pulled their pants up, and hurriedly crossed the street. Sam looked at April, and they laughed as they drove off.